"This ... you want to call it off."

"Call it off?" she repeated in a stark whisper.

Will nodded. "I don't like it, but I can accept that maybe this just isn't something you're willing to do. You can move back to the boardinghouse. We'll tell everyone we realized it wouldn't work, after all. But then, if there's a baby, I want you to promise me that you'll come back."

Call it off...

Did she want that?

They'd been "married" for just three days. Not only did Jordyn Leigh have to deal with her guilt over the lies they were telling, but sometimes when she told a lie, it came out seeming way too much like the truth.

The stuff she'd just said to Cece, for instance. About how wonderful Will was, how superhot and protective, how when he kissed her, she melted...

Well, she found it easy to tell those lies because those lies felt so very true.

It didn't seem possible. She didn't know how it had happened. But somehow, Will Clifton was beginning to look like her dream man.

* * *

MONTANA MAVERICKS:
WHAT HAPPENED AT THE WEDDING?
A weekend Rust Creek Falls will never forget!

Dear Reader,

What happened at the wedding? That's the big question these days in Rust Creek Falls, Montana.

At the Fourth of July wedding reception in Rust Creek Falls Park, a lot of people are kicking over the traces and doing things they've never done before. Will Clifton and Jordyn Leigh Cates are just two of the people whose lives will change forever because of what happens on Independence Day.

Will and Jordyn Leigh grew up together. He's five years older and has always treated her like a kid—until he spots her standing by the punch table in her blue bridesmaid's dress and realizes at last that little Jordyn Leigh is all grown up. He goes over to say hi—and never leaves her side for the rest of the afternoon and evening. Things get a little hazy as the night goes on, but still, it's the best time either of them has ever had.

And boy, are they in for a surprise come Sunday morning.

What happened at the wedding?

Will and Jordyn aren't really sure. But the wedding rings on their fingers and the marriage license by the bed would seem to indicate that they promised each other forever—whether they remember it or not!

Happy reading, everyone,

Christine Rimmer

The Maverick's Accidental Bride

Christine Rimmer

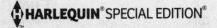
HARLEQUIN® SPECIAL EDITION®

Special thanks and acknowledgment to Christine Rimmer for her contribution to the Montana Mavericks: What Happened at the Wedding? continuity.

ISBN-13: 978-0-373-65895-4

The Maverick's Accidental Bride

Copyright © 2015 by Harlequin Books S.A.

Recycling programs for this product may not exist in your area.

This edition published by arrangement with Harlequin Books S.A.

For questions and comments about the quality of this book, please contact us at CustomerService@Harlequin.com.

Printed in U.S.A.

Christine Rimmer came to her profession the long way around. She tried everything from acting to teaching to telephone sales. Now she's finally found work that suits her perfectly. She insists she never had a problem keeping a job—she was merely gaining "life experience" for her future as a novelist. Christine lives with her family in Oregon. Visit her at christinerimmer.com.

Books by Christine Rimmer

Harlequin Special Edition

The Bravos of Justice Creek

Not Quite Married

The Bravo Royales

A Bravo Christmas Wedding
The Earl's Pregnant Bride
The Prince's Cinderella Bride
Holiday Royale
How to Marry a Princess
Her Highness and the Bodyguard
The Rancher's Christmas Princess

Bravo Family Ties

A Bravo Homecoming
Marriage, Bravo Style!
Donovan's Child
Expecting the Boss's Baby

Montana Mavericks: 20 Years in the Saddle!

Million-Dollar Maverick

Montana Mavericks: Rust Creek Cowboys

Marooned with the Maverick

Montana Mavericks: The Texans are Coming!

The Last Single Maverick

Visit the Author Profile page at Harlequin.com for more titles.

For MSR,
Always.

Chapter One

"You remind me of a girl I used to know," said a way-too-familiar deep voice in Jordyn Leigh Cates's ear. "She was just a kid, really. Pretty little thing, always following me around..."

Jordyn whirled on the killer handsome cowboy she'd known all her life. "Will Clifton, you liar. I never, *ever* followed you around."

"Yes, you did."

"Did not."

"Did so."

She laughed. "You know we sound like a couple of overgrown brats, right?"

"Speak for yourself." Will gave her the sexy half smile that had broken more than one girl's heart back home in Thunder Canyon. "Never could resist teasing you."

Jordyn sipped from her paper cup of delicious wedding punch. "I heard that you were in town."

"Craig, Jonathan and Rob, too." Those were his brothers.

"We're staying out at Maverick Manor." Formerly known as Bledsoe's Folly, the giant, long-deserted log mansion southeast of town had been transformed the year before into an upscale hotel with a rustic flair.

She gave him a teasing look from under her lashes. "I also heard a rumor that *you* bought a place right here in Rust Creek Falls...?"

"As a matter of fact, I did." There was real pride in his voice, and his gorgeous blue eyes shone bright with satisfaction. "Beautiful spread in the Rust Creek Valley, east of town, not far from the Traub ranch. Escrow closes on Tuesday."

Jordyn was happy for him. It had always been Will's dream to have his own ranch. "Congratulations."

"Thanks."

They grinned at each other. She thought he looked even hunkier than usual in a white dress shirt, a coffee-colored Western-cut vest and a bolo tie. He'd polished his belt buckle to a proud shine, and his black jeans broke just right over his black dress boots.

He reached out a hand and tugged on a blond curl that trailed loose from her updo. "You're lookin' good."

A warm lick of pleasure stole through her. He was five years her senior, and he'd always treated her like a kid. But right now, the way he gazed at her? She didn't feel like a kid in the least. She dared to flutter her eyelashes at him. "Thank you, Will."

He tipped his black Stetson. "It's only the truth. You look great—not to mention, patriotic."

"Red, white and blue all the way." She flicked a glance down at her strapless knee-length chiffon bridesmaid's dress. It was Old-Glory Blue.

Just a couple of hours ago, Braden Traub, second oldest of the Rust Creek Traub boys, had married angelic blonde

Jennifer MacCallum, who had moved to town a year before. They'd decided on an outdoor wedding reception—an Independence Day picnic in Rust Creek Falls Park. Red-and-white-checked oilcloths covered all the picnic tables. Red, white and blue canopies provided shade from the summer sun.

Plus, they'd set up a portable oak dance floor not far from the punch table, where Jordyn and Will stood. The six-piece band wasn't half bad. Right then they were rockin' a great Brad Paisley song. Jordyn's sparkly blue high heels had a tendency to get stuck in the grass when she wasn't out on the dance floor, but she refused to let that slow her down. She kept her weight on her toes and had no trouble tapping a foot to the music as a certain tall cowboy in a big white hat two-stepped by with a curvy brunette. That cowboy gave Jordyn a wink.

And Jordyn winked right back at him. "Wahoo, cowboy!" She raised her bridesmaid's bouquet of red roses in a jaunty wave.

And of course, Will just had to demand, "Who's that?"

She sent him a glance of serene self-possession. "Just a guy I was dancing with a little while ago…" What she didn't say was that she intended to be dancing with that cowboy again soon. Very soon. Will could get way too big-brotherly, and she didn't need that. She lifted her paper cup for another sip—and Will snagged it right out of her hand. "Hey!" She brandished her bouquet at him. "Give me back my punch, Clifton. Or I won't be responsible for what happens next."

He smirked at her and sniffed the cup. "What's in this, anyway?"

"Oh, please. It's just punch."

"Spiked?"

She puffed out her cheeks with a disgusted breath.

"Hardly. Punch, I said. Fruit juice and mixers—and a small amount of sparkling wine—and don't give me that look. I asked the bride so I know whereof I speak. It's a public park, Will. No hard liquor allowed."

Being Will, he just had to argue the point. "I've spotted a hip flask or two in the crowd."

"Well, yeah. But on the down low. The punch is harmless, believe me. And if you're so worried about a teeny bit of sparkling wine, try the kids' punch table." With a flourish, she pointed her bouquet at the table several feet away, where the children and teetotalers were served.

Will was watching her, his expression annoyingly suspicious. "You seem to be having a really good time, Jordyn Leigh—maybe *too* good a time."

"There is no such thing as too good a time." She scowled at him. "And do not call me Jordyn Leigh."

"Why not? It's your name."

"Yeah, but when *you* say it, I feel like I'm eight years old. Wearing hand-me-down jeans and a wrinkled plaid shirt, with my hair in pigtails and my two front teeth missing."

Looking right next door to wistful, Will shook his head. "I really liked that little girl."

"Well, I'm not her. And I haven't been for seventeen years." Right then, that weird old guy, Homer Gilmore, hobbled by on the other side of the punch table. He gave Jordyn a great big snaggle-tooth grin. Homer was as sweet as he was strange, so she responded with a merry wave. "I'm all grown-up now," she reminded Will.

"Yes, you are." He toasted her with her own cup and then drank the rest, bold as brass.

She could almost get aggravated that he'd commandeered her punch. But no. Back at the church during the wedding, she'd been feeling a tad low to be a bridesmaid and not a bride for the umpteenth time. But it was a beautiful day, not a cloud in the wide Montana sky. And hadn't she already shared a dance with a handsome cowboy? Who knew what good things might happen next? Her dark mood had vanished. Will was right. She was having a wonderful time. No way was she letting Will Clifton harsh her lovely mellow.

Instead, she grabbed a fresh flag-printed paper cup and poured herself another full one. When he held out the cup that used to be hers, she good-naturedly served him, as well.

They tapped cups and drank.

For Jordyn, the rest of that fateful afternoon flashed by in soft-focus snapshots.

She and Will hung out. And it was good. Better than good.

Up until that day, he'd always treated her like a youngster he needed to boss around. But from the first wedding-punch toast they'd shared that day, it was different.

Suddenly, they were equals. She had fun with him. A lot of fun. They ate barbecue and wedding cake together. They visited with his brothers, with the bride and groom, and with Jordyn's Newcomers Club girlfriends, who were also her fellow bridesmaids.

They met a quirky married couple, Elbert and Carmen Lutello. Elbert, small and thin with dark-rimmed glasses, was the county clerk. Carmen, broad-shouldered, commanding and a head taller than her husband, was a district judge. Carmen and Elbert were so cute together, totally dewy-eyed over each other—and the wedding and love and romance in general. Jordyn adored them.

She and Will enjoyed more punch. They danced together. Several dances. Somehow, she never got around to another dance with the cowboy in the white hat. Truth to tell, she forgot all about that guy. It was just her and Will, together in a lovely, misty place. The park, the picnic reception, the music and laughter…all that got pleasantly hazy around the edges, became background to the magic happening between her and Will.

Will kissed her. Right there on the dance floor. Just tipped her chin up with a finger and settled that sexy mouth of his on hers. They swayed to the music and kissed on and on.

Sweet Lord, the man could kiss. He kissed like the prince in a fairy tale, the kind of kiss that could wake a girl up from a hundred years of sleep. It was something of a miracle, the way Will kissed her that day. At last. Just when she'd started to doubt that she would ever be on the receiving end of kisses like his.

And he told her she was beautiful.

Didn't he?

It seemed he did. But she wasn't sure…

Not completely, anyway. Because things got hazier and hazier as the afternoon turned to evening.

Once night fell, a few weird things happened. One of the Dalton sisters got thrown in jail for resisting arrest—after dancing in the newly dedicated park fountain.

At some point Jordyn and Will stood hand in hand in the parking lot between Rust Creek Park and Brooks's Veterinary Clinic. They stared into the lambskin-lined trunk of Elbert Lutello's pink 1957 convertible Cadillac Eldorado Biarritz. Elbert hauled out a leather briefcase and announced with great solemnity, "You never know when a legal order or some other official form might be needed. I am a public servant, and I like to be prepared…"

And then, in the blink of an eye, Jordyn and Will, still holding hands, were swept magically back to the park with all the party lights twinkling beneath the almost-full moon. People crowded around them, watching. Carmen Lutello stood before them, blessing them with a tender smile.

What happened next?

Jordyn wasn't sure.

But the party went on. Will gave her more of those beautiful endless kisses; he fed them to her, each one delicious and perfect, filling her up with delight and satisfaction.

Actually, a lot of folks were kissing. You couldn't walk beneath a tree without having to ease around an embracing couple. And why not? It was only natural for everyone to be feeling happy and affectionate at a wedding. High spirits ruled on this special, joyous, romantic night...

The next morning, in her bed at Strickland's Boarding House, Jordyn woke to discover that an army of mean little men with pickaxes had taken up residence in her brain.

For several minutes, she lay very still with her eyes closed, waiting for her stomach to stop lurching and the little men with the axes to knock off attacking the inside of her skull. Finally, breathing slowly and evenly through her nose, she opened her eyes and stared at the ceiling.

The *wrong* ceiling...

Her pained grimace became a frown.

With great care, she turned her head toward the nightstand at her side. It was rustic, that nightstand, of what appeared to be reclaimed, beautifully worked old wood. It bore no resemblance to the simple pasteboard one she had at the boardinghouse. A clock stood on that nightstand—not her clock.

And wait a minute. How could it possibly be past noon?

Her stomach did a forward roll. She swallowed down a spurt of acid and carefully, torturously, rolled her head the other way.

Dear, sweet Mary and baby Jesus. *Will.*

She blinked, looked away—and looked back again.

He was still there, still sound asleep beside her, lying on his stomach with his face turned away from her, his hair night black against the white pillow. His strong arms and broad, muscular shoulders were bare. So was his powerful back tapering down to his tight waist. Below that, she couldn't be sure. The sheet covered the rest of him.

The sight of Will Clifton possibly naked right next to her in the bed that was not her bed was the final straw. Her stomach rebelled.

With a cry of abject wretchedness and total mortification, she threw back the covers and raced for the open door that led to the bathroom.

The slamming of the bathroom door woke Will.

With a loud "Huh?" he flipped to his back and bolted to a sitting position. "What the…?" He pressed both hands to his aching head and groaned.

But then he heard the painful sounds coming from the bathroom.

"Huh?" he said again. Apparently, he wasn't alone. There was someone in the bathroom. Someone being sick.

"Ugh." Still only half-awake, he raked the sleep-scrambled hair off his forehead. His gaze skimmed past the bedside chair—and then homed right back in on it.

His clothes from last night were tossed in a wad across that chair. On top of them, the hem drooping toward the floor, lay a pretty blue dress topped by a woman's small sparkly purse and a wilted red bouquet. Will shut his eyes as the heaving noises continued in the other room.

But then, well, keeping his eyes shut wouldn't make the sounds from the bathroom go away. So he opened them again—opened them and let them track lower, to the foot of the chair and the pair of sexy, sparkly, red-soled blue bridesmaid's shoes that had toppled sideways beneath the filmy hem of the blue dress.

Will knew that dress, those shoes, that bouquet…

Jordyn?

Jordyn Leigh Cates, in the bathroom? Sweet Jordyn Leigh, in his hotel room without her dress on? Little Jordyn Leigh…had spent the night in his *bed*?

He clapped his hands to his head again and tried to think it through.

Okay, he remembered spending the afternoon and evening with her yesterday. They'd had a great time.

But what had happened later? How did they get here to his hotel room together?

Damned if he could remember.

He threw back the covers and saw he was wearing only boxer briefs. Did that mean…?

Damn it all to hell. He had no idea what it meant.

And poor Jordyn. The sounds coming from the bathroom were not good.

He jumped to his feet and whipped his black jeans out from under her pretty blue dress. He was pulling them on as he hopped to the bathroom door. Zipping up fast, he gave the door a cautious tap. "Jordyn, are you—?"

She let out a low groan, a sound of purest misery. "Leave me alone, Will. Don't you dare come in here."

"Let me—"

"No! Stay there. I'll be out in a minute."

His head drooped forward until his forehead met the door. Jordyn Leigh? He'd had *sex* with little Jordyn Leigh? He wanted to beat the crap out of himself. Her younger brother, Brody, probably *would* beat the crap out of him— and he would deserve every punch. And what about her parents, who were good friends with *his* parents? Dear

God, he should be tied down spread-eagled in the noonday sun for the buzzards to peck to a million pieces. "Jordyn, I'm so sor—"

"Go *away*, Will!"

He raised his knuckles to knock again—but then just let them drop. "Uh. Just call. If you need me…"

She didn't bother to answer him that time. The heaving sounds continued.

He stood there, undecided, wanting to help, not knowing how. And that made him feel even more like a lowdown dirty dog, because he couldn't help and he knew it.

And he had no business just standing there, his head against the door, listening to her being sick.

So he dragged his sorry ass back to his side of the tangled bed and sat on the edge of it. He braced his elbows on his spread knees and let his head hang low in shame.

And that was when he spotted the document on the floor.

"Huh?" He picked it up.

Then, for a long time, several minutes at least, he just stared at the damn thing in stunned disbelief.

But it didn't matter how long he stared, the document didn't magically become something else. Uh-uh. No matter how long he stared, it was still a marriage license, complete with the embossed seal of the county clerk declaring it a true certified copy.

The county clerk…

Last night there was a guy, wasn't there? A little guy in black-rimmed glasses. Yeah. Elton or Eldred, something like that. And the little guy was married to that big woman, the judge…

Will blinked hard and shook his head. It didn't seem possible. He had zero recollection of any actual ceremony.

But still. He was reasonably sure the county clerk had been there last night, the county clerk and his wife, the judge.

So it *could* have happened. It *was* possible...

More than possible.

Because he held the proof right there in his two hands.

Around about then, he spotted the gleam of gold on the third finger of his left hand. Or maybe that gleam was brass. He couldn't be sure.

But gold or brass, the ring looked a hell of a lot like a wedding band. And that signature on the marriage license? Definitely his own. His—and Jordyn's, too.

It wasn't possible. But it *had* happened.

Somehow, he and Jordyn Leigh had gotten married last night.

Chapter Two

Will heard a click when Jordyn opened the bathroom door.

He set the marriage license on the nightstand by his side of the bed and slowly rose, turning to face the woman he'd apparently married the night before.

Jordyn Leigh stood in the doorway. Her big blue eyes had dark shadows beneath them. Her peaches-and-cream skin looked slightly green, and her soft mouth trembled.

She'd put on the complimentary terry-cloth robe that had been hanging on the back of the bathroom door. Her hands were stuck in the pockets, and she kept her head pulled in, like a turtle trying to retreat into its shell. Her wheat-gold hair lay smooth and wavy across her shoulders. She must have used his comb before opening the door and facing him at last.

The sight of all that shining hair made him feel worse than ever. It sent random images of her, scenes from their shared past, sparking and flashing through his brain.

He saw her as a toddler with wispy yellow curls, running through the sprinklers in her front yard, wearing a bright orange bathing suit that tended to sag around her little bottom. And then he saw her in pigtails and busted-out jeans at nine or ten, astride one of the Traub horses.

And the night of her prom...

He couldn't recall why he'd dropped by the Cates's place that night, but he did remember Jordyn Leigh, her hand on the banister, slowly descending the front hall stairs, wearing a pink satin dress, her hair piled up high, held in place with sparkling rhinestone clips.

She was such a sweet thing. She deserved so much better than this.

He cleared his throat. "Jordyn, I—"

But she whipped a hand free of a pocket and held it up to him, palm out. "I'm getting dressed right now, Will Clifton," she muttered through hard-clenched teeth. "I'm getting dressed and going back to the boardinghouse. And if you know what's good for you, you'll never tell a soul about this."

Okay, he might be a low-down skunk for...whatever had happened last night, but she ought to know him better than that. "Jordyn, I would never—"

"Hush!" She raised her chin high and smacked the air between them with her palm. "Don't, okay? Just don't." And then she gathered the robe closer at the neck. She did that with her left hand. He saw she wore no ring. But before he had time to consider what that might mean, she hunched into herself again and made a beeline for the chair and that blue bridesmaid's dress.

He moved fast, skirting the end of the bed, to intercept her before she reached the chair. "Jordyn, wait."

Folding her arms protectively around herself, she glared up at him. "Out of my way, Will." Her breath smelled of toothpaste.

He felt another stab of mingled guilt and regret as he pictured her brushing her teeth in the bathroom mirror with her finger and a dab of toothpaste, trying to gather her dignity around her, trying to be strong. He told her gently, "Before you go, we need to talk."

"Talking with you is the *last* thing I need." She tried to dodge around him.

But he caught her by the shoulders. "Hey, come on…"

"Let me go, Will." Her slim arms felt so delicate, so vulnerable, in his grip.

"Damn it, you're shaking."

"I'm fine."

"You are not."

"Am, too." She shook all the harder. He wanted to gather her close, but he feared that putting his arms around her would only freak her out all the more.

They had to discuss this reasonably, with cool heads. But she looked so sick and frantic. He was afraid if he sprung the big news that they somehow got married on her right then, she might just drop to the rug in a dead faint.

Or maybe she already knew they were married. Maybe *she* remembered what had actually happened…

But they would get to that. First, he needed to settle her down, maybe get some food into her.

She jerked in his grip. "Damn you, Will Clifton. You let me go."

But he didn't release her. Instead, he turned her and walked her backward to the bed. "I mean it, Jordyn Leigh. You need to sit down before you fall down." He gave her a gentle push.

And what do you know? Her knees gave out and she sank to the side of the bed. "Oh, dear Lord…" Her fake bravado deserted her. She let her shoulders slump and buried her head in her hands. "Oh, Will. What's going on? I don't remember...I don't..."

"Shh, settle down," he soothed. "Come on, put your feet up on the bed. Put your head on the pillow. Just, you know, rest a little, take it easy, okay?" Damned if she didn't do what he said for once. Obedient as the child she kept insisting she wasn't, she swung her feet up and stretched out. "Good," he whispered, and pulled up the covers nice and cozy around her. "Water?"

Blue eyes wide and worried, she bit her lip and nodded. He got a bottle of water from the minifridge. She sat up, and he propped the pillows behind her as she sipped.

"I'm thinking aspirin and room service first," he suggested. "Then we talk."

She gulped down more water. "Okay," she said in a tiny voice. "I could use some aspirin. And you're right. We should probably talk."

When the food came, Will served her in the bed.

Jordyn managed to get some dry toast and tea down, along with the aspirin. He moved their clothing from the chair to the sofa in the sitting area. Then he sat in the chair with his tray on his lap, shoveling in eggs, bacon, potatoes and a muffin, along with several cups of excellent Maverick Manor Blend coffee. By the third cup, he was feeling almost human.

Neither of them said much of anything while they ate. She avoided his gaze as she sipped her tea and nibbled her toast.

"Finished?" he asked finally. At her nod, he took her tray and put it with his outside in the hallway. He returned to the chair.

She smoothed her hair, though it didn't need it. And

then fiddled nervously with the sheet. "I don't even know where to start, Will. I remember the wedding—"

He blinked. "My God. You do?"

She looked at him like he maybe had a screw loose. "You're kidding? You actually thought I might have blacked out on the fact that Braden Traub and Jenny Mac-Callum got married yesterday?"

His racing heart slowed. "Uh. Right. Of course you remember that."

"What? *You* don't?"

"Oh, no. I do."

"Will. You're acting strangely."

Yeah, and why wouldn't he? It was a damn strange situation, after all. He watched as she plucked at the sheet some more. "Tell me what else you remember."

She straightened the front of the terry-cloth robe and blew out a slow breath. "I remember the reception in the park, or most of it. I think. I remember what happened in the afternoon. I remember us dancing..." She twisted the sheet. "But the later it got, the more it all just becomes one weird, hazy blur."

A sinister thought occurred to him, and he went ahead and shared it. "Maybe someone put something in your punch."

She went straight to denial on that idea. "Oh, no. No. I don't think so. Why would anyone do a thing like that?"

He regarded her patiently. "Why do you think?"

She wrinkled up her nose at him. "Oh, come on."

"It happens, Jordyn. We all like to think it doesn't. But what about that smart-ass cowboy in the white hat, the one who danced by and winked at you when we were first standing there at the punch table together?"

"He wasn't a smart-ass. He was really nice."

"Seemed like a smart-ass to me," Will muttered.

But she shook her head. "No. Uh-uh. I don't believe he would do a thing like that." She stared off toward the window that looked out over the hotel grounds.

"Don't just blow me off," he insisted. "Think about it. I drank from your cup after you did, remember? So maybe both of us were drugged—Jordyn, are you even listening?"

She met his eyes then, but hers were a thousand miles away. "I don't believe that guy drugged me. I just don't. He was a great guy."

"And you know this, how?"

She glanced away. "Okay, fine. He *seemed* like a great guy—and he never even had a chance to put anything in my drink. I danced with him once. He was nowhere near me when I served myself the punch."

"Are you sure?"

"Of course I'm sure. *You'd* have been more in a position to put something in my drink than anyone."

He gaped at her in horror. "Jordyn. You really don't think I would—"

"Of course not. And I don't think that other guy did, either." She'd stopped mangling the sheet—and gone to work wringing her hands. "And frankly, I'm more concerned with—" she turned away again and cleared her throat "—the question of whether or not you and I…" And then she looked at him again, her eyes huge and haunted. "Did we have sex, Will?"

Damn. Direct question. He tried to think of a gentle way to tell her that he had no idea if they had or they hadn't.

But he took too long, and she went on. "I hope *you* know, because *I* don't. I don't know how we got here, Will. It's all just vague, cloudy images, flashes of us dancing. Of us laughing together. Of us kissing…" Her too-pale face colored slightly.

He remembered those kisses, too, remembered that she

smelled so good and tasted so sweet, that her slim body fit just right in his arms. "I remember kissing you, too."

"So then tell me. Please. Did we...?"

He was forced to confess, "I'm sorry, Jordyn. But I don't remember, either."

She stared at him as though he'd just slapped her across the face. "Oh, fabulous." More color flooded her soft cheeks—angry color now. "So I'm that forgettable, am I?"

"Jordyn, be fair. You don't remember, either." He said it roughly, letting his own frustration show—and then regretted his harsh tone when her eyes welled with tears. "Aw, come on, don't cry..."

Too late. Fat tears spilled over and trailed down her cheeks. She sniffed. "I...I can't help it. I'm a virgin." His mouth dropped open when she said that. She let out a sad little sigh. "Or I *was* a virgin." He gaped at her as she swiped furiously at the tears running down her face. "Can you just not look at me like that, please?" She squeezed her eyes shut, but the tears still leaked out. "Oh, I can't believe I just said that, just *told* you that..."

He tried to soothe her. "Jordyn, it's okay..."

"It is *not* okay, and don't you say that it is. Everything is very, very *not* okay."

He pleaded, "You have to believe me. I can't see how I would ever take advantage of you that way." But he couldn't be sure, damn it. Because he just plain did not remember.

Jordyn cried harder. "Oh, look at me. What a mess. And now I've said it. Now you know. I was a virgin—or I *am* a virgin. That's what's so awful. I don't know if I am, or just was, because I can't remember what happened." And with that, she buried her head in her hands again. Her slim shoulders shook with desperate sobs.

Will had no idea what he ought to do to comfort her, so

he just sat there and watched her cry. He felt lower than low. Not only had he possibly had sex with little Jordyn Leigh—if he had, she'd also been a virgin.

He didn't have sex with virgins. He knew better than that.

Still sobbing, Jordyn shoved back the covers, scooted aside and stared at the sheets. "Nothing, no blood," she said with a moan as she tugged on the hem of the robe. Then she whipped a few tissues from the box by the clock, blew her nose and declared, "I don't see any blood, and I don't *feel* like anything happened." She tossed the used tissues toward the wastebasket, flipped the covers over her again and folded her arms across her middle.

Silence. Jordyn gazed into space. Will had no idea what she might be thinking.

But he needed to comfort her. He needed to wipe that lost look off her pretty face. So in the interest of injecting a positive note into this train wreck of a situation, he blurted, "Listen, it could be worse. If we did make love last night, at least we were married first."

She missed the positive angle altogether and screeched, "Married? Have you lost your mind?" And she whipped one of the pillows from behind her and tossed it at his head. He put up both hands and caught it before it hit him in the face—at which point Jordyn screeched again. "Oh, my God! Will! Your finger!"

He peered cautiously around the pillow at her. "Huh?"

"You've got a ring on your ring finger, too!"

He just wasn't following. *Too?*

She muttered something discouraging under her breath, tossed back the covers again and jumped to her feet.

"Jordyn," he asked warily, "where are you going now?"

She didn't answer, just headed for the bathroom. A moment later she returned, plunked herself down on the side of the bed and held up a ring like the one he wore, only smaller. "It freaked me out when I saw it on my finger," she confessed glumly. "So I took it off and stuck it under a stack of extra towels." She dropped it on the nightstand. It spun for a moment and then settled. Jordyn cut her eyes to him again. "I don't remember getting married...though maybe, well, I do remember that little man with the black-rimmed glasses. He was the county clerk. Do you remember him?"

"I do. I remember him *and* his wife, the judge..."

She nodded, her eyes staring blankly into the middle distance again. "I stood beside you, Will. I remember that. I stood beside you under the moon. We were holding hands, and people were all around us, and Her Honor, the judge, was in front of us. And after that..."

"Yeah?"

A long, sad sigh escaped her. "After that, it's all a blank."

He couldn't bear to see her looking so dejected, so he got up and went to her. She didn't jump away when he sat down beside her, and that gave him the courage to wrap an arm around her. "You have to look on the bright side."

She made a doleful sound. "There's a bright side?"

"Yes, there is. Think about it. You saved yourself for marriage—and, well, *if* we had sex, we have proof that we were married at the time."

At first, she said nothing, only eased out from under his sheltering arm and faced him. Her expression was not encouraging. Finally, she demanded, "*That's* the bright side?"

He knew he'd stepped in it again. He gulped. "Er, it's not?"

Proudly, she informed him, "You don't get it, Will. It's not marriage I was waiting for. It's love. Or if not love, then at least *special*."

He nervously scratched the side of his neck. "Ahem. *Special?*"

"Yes. Special. That's what I waited for, something really special with a special, special man. And I have to tell you that having sex with you while unconscious is not the kind of special I was going for—plus, just because we woke up with rings on doesn't mean we're *really* married. Don't you need a license to be *really* married?"

He gave her a long look as he wondered if he should even go there. And then he threw caution to the wind and asked, "So if there was a license, you would believe that our marriage was real?"

She narrowed her eyes at him. "Is that a trick question?"

"Stay right there."

"Where are you going?" she demanded crossly as he got up, turned around and crawled across the mattress. "What are you *doing*?"

He crawled back, swung his legs to the floor so he was sitting beside her again—and held out the marriage license. "Believe it. It's real."

Jordyn read the document over several times before she could let herself believe what she was seeing.

Again, she remembered the skinny little clerk and his pink Cadillac, that briefcase where he kept those official documents. He could so easily have kept a box of cheap rings in there, too…

Will said, "So you see. I think it's real. I think we really are married."

Married. To Will Clifton.

She looked up into his worried eyes—and knew she couldn't bear another minute, another second of sitting there beside him trying to pin down what, exactly, had happened last night. "Here." She shoved the license at him.

"I've had enough." She jumped to her feet, ran to the sofa in the sitting area and snatched up her dress and shoes from where he'd set them before they ate.

"Jordyn, come on. We need to stay calm. We need to—"

"Stop talking, Will."

"But—"

"Stop. Please. I can't take any more. I've got to get dressed. I've got to get out of here." And with that, she ran into the bathroom and shut and locked the door.

"The county courthouse and offices are closed for the three-day weekend." Will eased his quad cab to the curb in front of Strickland's Boarding House. "They open again tomorrow. First thing in the morning, we'll head for Kalispell and straighten this craziness out. Maybe that license isn't even filed yet. Maybe we can make this whole thing just go away."

Jordyn stared out the windshield. For the moment, the street was quiet. No kids out playing, no neighbors working in their yards or walking their dogs. If she moved fast, she might get up the steps and in the front door before anyone spotted her going in wearing the same blue dress and high heels she'd been wearing the night before.

Will caught her arm as she leaned on the door handle. "Jordyn. Tomorrow?"

She gulped and nodded. "Yes. Tomorrow morning. Okay."

He stared in her eyes as though looking for a sign from her—but a sign of what? She had no clue. His cell started ringing, which was great because he let her go.

"Tomorrow," he said again, the phone already at his ear.

She made her escape, jumping to the sidewalk, shoving the door shut and then turning to sprint along the walk and up the stairs of the ramshackle four-story Victorian. She had her key out and ready when she hit the door. All she wanted was to get in and get up the two sets of stairs to her room on the third floor without having to talk to a soul.

But no.

As she fumbled to stick the key in the lock, the door swung open. Sweet old Melba Strickland, who owned and ran the boardinghouse, stood on the other side wearing one of those floral-patterned dresses she favored and a pair of very sensible shoes. Melba was at least eighty, but spry. She had a warm heart, a willing hand—and a staunch moral code.

Melba believed in the power of love. She also believed that sex should only occur between two people married in the sight of God and man. She'd made it way clear from Jordyn's first day at the rooming house almost two years ago now that there would be no hanky-panky on the premises. Yes, it was the twenty-first century, and Melba's old-fashioned ideas didn't stop her tenants from hooking up, anyway. They just did it discreetly.

Coming home in the middle of the afternoon in last night's bridesmaid's dress, looking like something the cat dragged in?

Not exactly discreet.

"Honey, are you all right?" Melba took Jordyn's hand and pulled her inside. "When you didn't come down for breakfast, I assumed you just needed a little extra sleep after the big party last night. By eleven or so, though, I began to worry. You're not the kind to sleep half the day away." Jordyn saw no judgment in Melba's eyes—nothing but affection and honest concern.

Again, the image of her and Will in front of Carmen Lutello last night rose up in her mind's eye. Had Melba been there?

No. If she had, she would have known why Jordyn didn't come down for breakfast. Plus, it had happened pretty late in the evening, hadn't it? Melba and her husband, Old Gene, rarely stayed up past ten.

Melba patted her hand. "Darling, what's wrong? What's happened? You look so pale."

"I'm all right," she baldly lied. "There's nothing wrong."

"Have you eaten?" The old woman started herding Jordyn toward the arch to the dining room.

"I had some tea and toast." Gently, Jordyn eased free of Melba's grip. "I'm not hungry."

"You sure, now?"

"Yes. I'll, um, be down later and get something then." She headed for the stairs and took them at a near run, never once pausing or glancing back until she'd reached the third-floor landing, where she halted, breathing fast, her stomach roiling, listening for the sound of Melba's sensible shoes coming up behind her.

But Melba stayed below. With a sigh of relief, Jordyn hurried along the third-floor hall to her room. She'd barely shut the door and sagged against it when her cell started ringing.

"What now?" She dug it out of her clutch and tossed the clutch on the dresser nearby. The display read *Will*. Just *Will*. She couldn't remember having Will's cell number— and if she had, she'd have programmed in his last name.

Which was now *her* last name.

"Oh, God." With an unhappy moan, she answered it. "How did you get my number?"

"I have no idea. I'm guessing we probably exchanged numbers last night."

"Of course." They'd exchanged so much last night. Phone numbers. Wedding vows. Possibly bodily fluids. She moaned again.

"Jordyn, are you okay?"

"No, I am not. Where *are* you, Will?"

"Out in front, in my pickup."

"Why aren't you gone yet?"

"Because I got a call from Craig." Craig was the oldest of Will's brothers.

"Why does that sound like very bad news?"

"Look. I just think you should know. Craig was there last night, when we got married. So was half the town, apparently."

Half the town? Lovely. Half the town knew more than she did about what she and Will had done last night. "I know there were people there. I told you that. This isn't news, Will."

"Yeah, it kind of is." He sounded scarily grim.

She kicked off her sparkly shoes and slid down the door till her butt hit the floor. "Just tell me."

"Craig says everyone's talking about it, about the ceremony in the park, about our, um, smoking-hot kiss—you know, the one that sealed our vows?"

Her headache had come back. With a vengeance. "So we kissed. Of course we kissed. That's what you do when you get married. Is that all?"

"Er, no."

"Then what else?"

"We made the *Rust Creek Falls Gazette*."

"What are you talking about, Will? I don't understand…"

"Apparently, there's this column called Rust Creek Ramblings written by some mystery gossip columnist. Does that ring a bell?"

Nobody knew who the columnist was, but he or she always had the scoop, was always outing the personal, intimate and romantic business of people in town. A low moan escaped Jordyn. "Oh, no…"

"Yeah. Craig says this morning's column is all about

you and me. All about our surprise wedding. It's, uh, not all that flattering, Craig says."

"Not all that flattering. What does that *mean*?"

"I'm not sure yet. I'm going to go get a copy of the *Gazette* and find out."

Jordyn cast a longing glance at her bed with its pretty white eyelet bedspread. All she wanted at that moment was to get in and pull the covers over her head.

"Jordyn, we really need to talk some more. We need to give careful consideration to how we want to handle this. We have to—"

"Will."

"Yeah?"

"I need some rest." She was going to take a hot shower, crawl under the covers and not come out for a year.

"All right," he said resignedly.

"Thank you."

And then he just *had* to remind her, "Tomorrow. First thing. We're going to Kalispell, remember? I'll pick you up at eight."

"I remember. I'll be ready." She hung up.

About then, it occurred to her that she was expected at work tomorrow. She would need the day off, and the sooner she called in, the better. She autodialed Sara, one of her two bosses at Country Kids Day Care Center.

"This is Sara Johnston."

"Hi, Sara, it's Jordyn Leigh."

"Hey! What a party yesterday, huh? I hear congratulations are in order…"

Jordyn, still on the floor in front of the door, put a soothing hand on her iffy stomach and wished her head would stop hurting. "I, um, yeah. Thank you. It was something, wasn't it?" she offered lamely.

"I just wish I'd been there. Suzie told me." Suzie Johnston was Sara's twin sister and her partner in the day care. "Suzie said it was so romantic, and you and your new husband looked so happy together. He's from Thunder Canyon, I understand. Just like you."

"Uh, yeah. I've known him since we were kids."

"He's one of Cecelia's brothers, right?" Cecelia Clifton Pritchett used to live at Melba's boardinghouse, too. So had Cece's new husband, Nick. Sara said, "His name's Will, right?"

"That's right—and Sara, listen, I called because I kind of need to take the day off tomorrow…" Jordyn's voice trailed off as she realized that she would have to tell Sara something about why she needed the day. She gathered her courage to explain everything.

But Sara believed that Jordyn was a real newlywed. "Take the week, if you need it. Be with your new hubby. Enjoy every minute. Have yourselves a honeymoon, for goodness' sake."

"You're an angel." *And I ought to have the integrity to tell you the truth.* But she didn't. She couldn't. Not right now. She'd deal with all that later. "I just need tomorrow. I'll be in Tuesday."

"You're sure?"

"Positive."

"If you change your mind, just call. We can manage if you need the time."

"Thanks so much."

"You're so welcome—and Jordyn Leigh, you be happy, you and your new husband, you hear? It all goes by so fast, believe me." Sara's voice held the weight of sadness now. She'd lost her husband in a car accident when their youngest was only a baby. "You need to treasure every moment the good Lord gives you together."

"Thanks, Sara. I will." The good Lord was probably up in heaven shaking His head.

Still, Jordyn let Sara believe what she wanted to. Eventually, the moment of truth would come, and Jordyn would face it. At least by then she'd be done with this awful hangover.

Sara said goodbye at last. Jordyn disconnected the call, dragged herself to her feet, grabbed her shower caddy and her robe and headed for the bathroom at the end of the hall.

Feeling pretty damn bad about everything, Will drove the two blocks to Crawford's General Store to get a copy of the *Rust Creek Falls Gazette*. The coin-operated rack by the entrance was empty, so he went inside to ask where else to get a paper.

Mrs. Crawford had a stack of them by the register. She took his money and congratulated him on his marriage. "I hope you and Jordyn Leigh will be very happy together." She seemed sincere enough.

Will thanked her, stuck the paper under his arm and turned to go. But he just happened to walk down the center aisle on his way out, the one lined with canned goods of every variety.

Two middle-aged ladies stood chatting in that aisle. One was tall and heavyset, the other thin with gray hair pulled back into a tight little bun. They didn't see him coming, they were so wrapped up in gossiping together.

The tall one clucked her tongue. "It's a disgrace is what it is. Two virtual strangers, that's what I heard." Will hesitated several feet away, dread creeping like a spider down his spine. Neither lady turned to see him standing there. The tall one went on, "They got married in a drunken stupor right there in Rust Creek Park at eleven o'clock last night."

The thin one said, "I heard that the *blushing* bride is one of those desperate Gal Rush women. Came to town looking for a husband during reconstruction after the flood."

"Well, and now she's caught one."

"Hah. But not for long, I'll bet. My guess is the groom's probably already running for the hills like his hair's on fire."

The tall one chortled merrily.

And Will knew he couldn't let that stand. So what if he and Jordyn *were* planning to end their unexpected marriage ASAP? Didn't matter. He wasn't standing by and having the sweet, spunky girl he'd grown up with disrespected.

"It's a disgrace to the institution of marriage," declared the thin one with an angry sniff.

That did it. Will walked right up to them. "Excuse me, ladies." He tipped his hat. Looking startled, they both turned to stare at him. He said, "It so happens that you are misinformed."

"Well, I never..." said the tall one.

"Really?" The thin one sneered.

"Yes," he said. "Really. You see, I'm the groom you were just now discussing." He offered the tall one his hand. "Will Clifton." She took it limply then quickly let go. "Pleased to meet you." He gave her his warmest smile and turned to the skinny one. "Ma'am." The thin one blinked several times in rapid succession before briefly taking his offered hand.

As soon as she released his fingers, Will swept off his hat and pressed it to his heart. "Have a good look now, ladies." He tipped his chin down so they had a clear view of every hair on his head. "Not a spark, not an ember, not one whiff of smoke. My hair is not on fire, so you got that all wrong. As a matter of fact, I'm a local now. I've bought the old Dodson place east of town. I'm going nowhere. Why would I want to? Rust Creek Falls is my home. And that's not all. I don't know where you've been getting your information, but someone has been telling you lies. Because my new wife and I did not marry impulsively."

Well, who was to say about that? Neither he nor Jordyn remembered their exact states of mind at the time they'd said their vows.

He continued, "Jordyn Leigh and I are both from Thunder Canyon. We are by no means strangers to one another. In fact, we've known each other since we were children. Our families are very good friends. I'm the happiest man in the world right now, because I love my wife with all my heart, and the day has finally come when she is mine."

Yeah, all right. The love stuff was total crap. But so what?

It worked.

The tall lady sputtered out, "Well, I…erm…" and then couldn't figure out what to say next.

The thin one looked like she'd swallowed a lemon.

Will put his hat back on. "Real nice to meet you ladies. Have a great day, now." He took his *Gazette* out from under his arm, gave them a final wave with it and headed for the door.

Once back in his quad cab, he dropped the paper on the passenger seat and got the hell out of there. A few minutes later, he was pulling into the parking lot at Maverick Manor a few miles down the highway, southeast of town. He didn't open that paper until he was safe in his room.

The gossip column was a long one. It covered a lot more strange goings-on than what had happened between him and Jordyn. Others had behaved badly last night, and the mystery columnist hadn't hesitated to lay it all out there in black-and-white, including the waitress who went swimming in the park fountain and ended up in jail for it, and also a poker game at the local watering hole, where one of the Crawford boys won somebody's ranch.

The part about Will and Jordyn came last. Unlike those two awful ladies in Crawford's, the column was not cruel. Looked at objectively, he supposed the story of his spur-of-the-moment marriage might even seem romantic. But the fact remained that he hated to have a spotlight shone on the night he could barely remember—and he knew that Jordyn would hate it, too. In the end, what were they but two moonstruck idiots who'd lost their heads and tied the knot?

Frankly, reading it pissed Will off. No, it wasn't mean-spirited. But come on. Whoever wrote it should at least have had the guts to put their name to it. And didn't that columnist even wonder what had gotten into everyone last night?

Will did. He still suspected that cowboy in the white hat of spiking their punch. And beyond the issue of who put what in Jordyn's punch, the column and the encounter with the two ladies in Crawford's store had him rethinking what to do next.

Because they *were* married, and everyone seemed to know it. And in a town like Rust Creek Falls, people took their wedding vows seriously. If he and Jordyn didn't find the right way to deal with this accidental marriage of theirs, she would be shamed before the whole town, and he wouldn't look like much of a man.

The more he reconsidered their situation, the more certain he became that he and Jordyn needed a better plan than just to race off to Kalispell to see if they could call the whole thing off. Because it was too damn late for that.

Chapter Three

In the morning, when Will pulled up in front of the boardinghouse, Jordyn Leigh was waiting on the front steps wearing faded jeans and a little white T-shirt. She jumped up and ran down the steps to meet him, the morning sun picking up glints of bronze and auburn in her pale gold hair.

"Hey." She gave him a nod and a wobbly attempt at a smile as she pulled the passenger door shut. A hint of her scent came to him, that pleasing perfume he remembered from Saturday night, like flowers and spring grass and ripe, perfect peaches.

"Mornin'," he said.

She plunked her bag at her feet, hooked up her seat belt and stared straight ahead.

He put it in gear and off they went. "You sleep okay?"

She sent him a look that said, *Are you kidding?* And then she went back to her intense study of the street ahead of them.

Once they got to the highway, he tried to get her talking—about harmless things. About the weather and her job at the local day care. But she was having none of it. Her answers consisted of as few words as possible. She volunteered nothing.

He went ahead and asked her if she'd seen the *Gazette*. "I saw it," she answered. That was it. Nothing more.

He kept trying. "I talked to Craig again last night. He had more on the Brad Crawford story—Brad's the guy who won that ranch in the poker game." He waited for a nod or a grunt from her to tell him she was listening. Nothing. He soldiered on. "Well, now the ranch belongs to Brad, and the former owner has vanished into thin air. Nobody's seen him since Saturday night. Some folks are thinking there's been foul play."

Jordyn only shrugged and stared out the windshield.

Will gave it up. For the time being, anyway. They rode the rest of the way in silence.

In Kalispell, it only took a few minutes to get to the county justice center. Will parked in the lot, and they went in together. The county clerk's office was on the third floor. They waited their turn in line and quickly learned that the clerk himself wasn't in the office right then.

At that news, Jordyn muttered, "Thanks a bunch, Elbert."

The woman who helped them told them that yes, their license was on file and they were indeed married. As Jordyn stood wide-eyed and silent at his side, Will went ahead with the original plan and asked about the possibility of an annulment.

The woman clucked her tongue as if in sympathy and then patiently explained that it would actually be very difficult for them to get an annulment. "In Montana, an annulment requires proof that there has been no sexual intercourse between the married couple. You can imagine how complicated proving that can be."

Jordyn made a strangled sound. Will fully expected her to burst into tears, and he braced to deal with that.

But somehow she held it together, and the woman went right on, "What you want is a joint dissolution—joint dissolution meaning that you two file jointly for your divorce. It's simple and straightforward and also fair." She gave them the large packet of documents they would need and said that the same documents were also available to print off online.

"Fill them out completely and bring them back," she said. "When you return all the needed documentation—in person, together—you'll be given a hearing date a maximum of twenty days out. The hearing is a formality. Bottom line, twenty days from filing jointly, you will be divorced."

They went back downstairs and out the door. Back in the quad cab, Jordyn remained scarily subdued.

Will tried again to get through to her. "Jordyn. I think we really need to talk some more about all this."

But she only shook her head. "Just take me back to the boardinghouse, please."

He drove north on Main and turned right on Center. Two blocks later, he pulled into the parking lot of a cute little café. The tidy building was painted white, and there were cheerful geraniums in cast-iron boxes at each of the wide windows. He switched off the engine and stuck his key in his pocket.

Jordyn shook off her funk long enough to send him a scowl. "What are you doing, Will?"

"I need some breakfast. Did you eat?"

Her eyes flashed with annoyance. "I told you, I want to go back to the boardinghouse."

He slid his arm along the back of the seat and leaned a little closer to her. "So you didn't eat."

She just stared at him, her soft lower lip beginning to quiver.

He wanted to reach out and pull her close and tell her it was going to be all right. But he had a very strong feeling that if he so much as touched her, she would shatter. So he kept his hands to himself and said reasonably, "We need to eat. And we also need to talk."

She bit her lip. And then at last, she nodded. "Okay," she said in a voice that only shook a little. "We'll eat. And you're right. We should talk."

Jordyn followed Will into the cheery little restaurant. She really didn't want to be there. She felt so awful about everything, and Will was being so wonderful and calm and reasonable and understanding.

She wanted to grab him and hug him tight and tell him how great he was. But if she did, she would only end up blubbering like a big baby, and that would only make it all crappier than ever.

Dear Lord, they were *married*. They were really, truly married. And now they would have to get divorced. Jordyn didn't believe in divorce. In her family, marriage was forever.

It was all so wrong.

She felt caught in some awful nightmare, one she couldn't seem to make herself wake up from.

Will chose a table in the corner. The waitress came and poured them coffee. He ordered steak and eggs, and Jordyn opened her mouth to say she only wanted the coffee. But Will's beautiful blue eyes were on her, giving her that look, both stern and gentle, so she ordered a pancake sandwich.

They sipped their coffee in silence until the food came.

He dug right in. She drizzled syrup on her pancakes and nibbled at the bacon and felt a ray of hope that maybe he'd given up on the idea that their accidental marriage demanded further discussion.

But he hadn't given up. Once he'd worked his way through half his steak and two of his three eggs, he leaned across the table toward her and said, low-voiced so it stayed just between the two of them, "We need a better plan."

She set down her half-eaten strip of bacon. "Better, how?"

He ate more steak, sipped his coffee. "I know you're upset about this, Jordyn, and I don't want to make it any worse than it already is for you, but have you thought about what to do if it turns out you're pregnant?"

Her stomach lurched. She pushed her barely touched plate away and confessed in a whisper, "No. I… Oh, my God." The thought that she might be pregnant hadn't even occurred to her.

"I'm going to just lay it out there." He held her gaze, steadily.

She coughed into her hand weakly, trying to clear the sudden lump from her tight throat. "All right."

"I carry a condom in my wallet. It's still there."

"Oh," she said, because she had no idea what else to say.

One black eyebrow lifted. "You're not by any chance on the pill?" When she shook her head, he suggested, "So maybe you want to get that Plan B pill, just in case?"

Jordyn shook her head again. "I don't believe I'm pregnant. And as for that Plan B pill…no. Just no. I'm not going there."

Now Will wore his most patient expression. "All right. But you have to see that we can't be sure about anything. It's possible we had sex Saturday night. And if we did, then it's possible that you're pregnant."

Her cheeks suddenly felt on fire. She pressed her hands against them to cool the flash of heat. "What do you want from me, Will?"

"You really want to know?" He waited for another nod from her before he said, "I think we need to stay married for a while."

"But I don't—"

"Wait. Hear me out."

She pulled her coffee mug closer and wrapped her hands around it, seeking comfort from the warmth of it, from its curving, firm shape. "Go on."

"Jordyn, if you're having my baby, there will be no divorce. If there's a baby, I want your agreement that we'll find a way to make this marriage work."

Oh, she did long to argue—that it was all a crazy nightmare, that a baby wasn't possible.

But no. She needed to snap out of this numb state of denial she'd been dragging around in since she woke up in Will's bed yesterday. They'd done…whatever they'd done on Saturday night. And if there was a baby, well, she and Will shared the same values. If there was a baby, they *would* make it work. "Okay, you're right. I agree. About the baby. I mean, if there is one, we'll stay married."

He let out a slow breath. "Good."

"But I'm sure there's not."

"Be sure all you want, Jordyn. It's still possible, and we have to accept that."

She longed to make him—to make *somebody*— understand. "I…well, I do have plans, Will. I know people think I just came to Rust Creek Falls to get myself a man—and maybe I did. A little. Because the truth is I am sort of a hopeless romantic."

He slathered strawberry jam on a triangle of toast.

"There's nothing the least bit hopeless about you, Jordyn Leigh."

His rueful words warmed her, deep down, where she needed warmth most right then. "Not hopeless, then." She dared a smile. He gave her a grin in return. "But I *am* a romantic. I believe in love and marriage and family and forever. I believe in waiting for that one special man. And I guess that's why what we did Saturday night—whatever it was—has me wanting to climb in my bed and hide under the covers. What we did flies hard in the face of everything I believe."

"I know that." He held her gaze in that unwavering way he had. "But we still have to deal with it the best way we can."

"I know. I agree. And what I'm trying to say is, yes, I'm a romantic. I want real love and a true marriage. I'm... disappointed that I haven't found the right guy when all four of my sisters are married and settled down, when everyone else seems to be coupled up and getting on with their lives. I'm disappointed, but I'm not giving up living over it. I haven't been just sitting around waiting for some guy to show up and give my life meaning. I have plans of my own. Career plans."

He ate another bite of steak. "Tell me about those plans."

She sent him a sideways look. "You really want to know?"

"I do, absolutely."

Did he mean that? He seemed to. She took him at his word. "Okay, then. I've been taking classes online, and I'm only a couple of semesters away from a degree in child development. I thought, well, okay. It didn't work out for me in Rust Creek Falls. I've made good friends there and I've loved living there. But the true, forever love I hoped to find when I moved to town never showed up. So I decided it was time to try something new, you know? Time to get out in the big world and make my mark."

"So...?"

"So I'm off to Missoula, to UMT, in the fall. I'm all enrolled and ready to go. I have a little money from Grandpa Cates, and I've saved enough to manage it, as long as I find a job once I get there. So I do have a plan. I have a dream, Will, I really do. I want to get my degree and have a meaningful, productive career. I'm leaving Rust Creek Falls at the end of August. And I don't care what a few small-minded people there say."

He set down his knife and fork and slowly shook his head. "I don't believe you. I think you do care. And *I* care. I don't accept that you should ever have to feel shamed or embarrassed by what happened Saturday night. And even if you're leaving, *I* live in Rust Creek now. I want to be known as a man who honors his commitments."

"But if it's not a *real* commitment—"

"It *is* a real commitment." He said it roughly, almost angrily. "We *are* actually married. No, it's probably not going to last forever. But it is a commitment that we should both take seriously, that we need to treat with respect and dignity. I've said it before. We need a better plan. And I have one, a plan that will keep other people out of our business, a plan that doesn't necessarily have to interfere with your going to college."

She gulped. "You do?"

"Yeah. When did you say your fall term starts?"

"Orientation is second-to-last week of August."

"That should work fine."

"Uh, it should?"

"We'll stay married through the summer. You'll move in with me at my new place."

That had her sitting up good and straight. "Tell me you didn't just say that I would move in with you."

"That is exactly what I said. You'll move in at the ranch, and if anyone asks about your college plans, you'll tell them all about how proud and supportive I am of you, how I've insisted you have your education, that it's your lifetime dream, and I intend for you to have your dream."

She tried to make a joke of it. "Gee, what a guy. I think you're my hero."

He didn't miss a beat. "You'll say how, even though you're going to UMT this fall, you'll be coming home often, because we hate to be apart."

"I will?"

He nodded. "How long until you know if you're pregnant?"

"You know, I think we ought to slow down a little here and—"

"How *long*, Jordyn?"

She knew that mulish look. He would be keeping after her until she answered him. "Oh, fine. A couple of weeks, I guess. I'm, um, pretty regular. Or I can probably take a home test sooner than that."

"Say a couple of weeks, then, just for a reference point. If you *are* having a baby, we'll figure out a way to make the marriage work. If not, we'll file the papers at the end of July, and we'll be divorced by the time you leave for Missoula."

She fiddled with the salt shaker. "I'm just not sure this is such a good idea."

"Well, *I* am. Questions?"

She had a powerful urge to bop him upside his thick head. "As a matter of fact, I do have a question."

"Hit me with it."

Oh, I wish. "Do you mean for us to share a room?"

He looked vaguely offended. "Jordyn. You know me better than that. I'm trying to *help* you, not put a move on you."

"I think I would be better off just to be honest with everyone and deal with the fallout—and move on."

The man did not miss a beat. "Well, you're wrong. *My* way is better for both of us—and where was I? Oh, yeah. Separate rooms. But everywhere except in bed, we would be together, making it work."

"But it would be a lie, Will. We would be lying to everyone."

"No, we wouldn't. Because we really are married. And it's nobody's business but ours how we choose to *be* married. And if it did turn out that you were pregnant, we would already have a life together. Think about that. Think about our innocent child."

A wild laugh bubbled up inside her, and she couldn't quite hold it back.

Those black brows drew together. "What's so funny?"

"It's just…*you*, Will. Determined to protect my reputation, so set on doing what you consider the right thing. I mean, we don't even know if we had sex, yet you're already talking about protecting the baby."

He looked a tad insulted. "Exactly. On all counts. What of it?"

"So…I would pay you rent?"

He scowled. "Of course not."

"But if I'm going to be staying at your place—"

"You mind doing some of the cooking, keeping things tidy, generally helping out around the house?"

"Of course I don't mind, but I should still pay you—"

He cut her right off again. "You help out where needed. That's more than enough payment for me. Believe me, there will be plenty of work to do. And the house has three bedrooms. I can only use one myself."

A minute ago she'd been laughing. She wasn't laughing now. She held his gaze across the table and silently admitted to herself that she really had been dreading facing everyone alone, being a joke, a laughingstock. "Some people will still gossip," she warned.

"So what? Let 'em talk. They'll get bored with it pretty quick when they see that we're just a nice, happily married couple. They'll have to find something else to talk about."

"I just..."

The waitress appeared. She refilled their coffee mugs. "Can I get you two anything else?"

"A check." Will waited as the woman pulled the bill from her apron and set it on the table. She scooped up his empty plate and moved on. He regarded Jordyn silently for a second or two before prompting, "You just, what?"

She forked her fingers through her hair. "Are you sure you really want to do this?"

"It's *my* plan. You bet I'm sure."

Jordyn marveled at him. She thought back to all those years growing up, when he used to thoroughly annoy her with his overbearing know-it-all big-brother act. She probably should have appreciated him more. If she had to be accidentally married to someone, it helped that she'd chosen a guy who'd always looked out for her, a guy who wanted the best for her, one who intended to stand up for her, stand up *with* her, until she left Rust Creek Falls behind. "You're one of the good guys, Will, a real hero. And I mean that sincerely this time."

"Just say that you'll do it." His quiet voice was gruff.

And even though she still had her doubts, the possibility that there might be a baby had tipped the scales for her. "All right, yes. Let's do it. Let's go ahead with your plan."

There was a silence. They stared into each other's eyes. Finally, he said, "Give me your hand."

She reached across the table to him.

"Uh-uh. Your *left* hand." He dipped into the breast pocket of his Western-style shirt—and came out with the wedding band she'd abandoned on the nightstand in his room the day before.

Tears burned behind her eyes at the sight of it. Suddenly, the moment seemed filled with meaning. Her heart ached—but in a good way, really. "Leave it to you to think of everything."

His fine mouth quirked. "Your hand, Jordyn Leigh."

So she held out her hand, and he slipped that ring back on her finger. And then she found she was reaching with her other hand, too. He met her halfway. They held hands across the table.

"Thank you," she whispered in a voice that only wobbled a little bit.

Chapter Four

On the way back to Rust Creek Falls, he kept shooting her glances out of the corner of his eye.

She knew he was working up to something. "Okay, Will. Whatever it is, you might as well just say it."

He shot her another glance then stared at the road again.

She gave it a mental count of ten before she prodded, "Still waiting. Better just tell me."

"Ahem. About tonight…"

She folded her arms across her middle. "What about it?"

A swift, measuring glance, then, "This is my last night at the Manor. Tomorrow I take possession of my ranch."

"Right. You told me that Saturday—before we did a whole lot of crazy stuff and then forgot about half of it."

"I think you need to stay with me."

"We already agreed on that."

"No, Jordyn. I mean tonight. In my room. We're married, remember? We need to play to that."

She thought about arguing—that she'd slept at the

boardinghouse last night, that one more night wouldn't matter that much. That they'd agreed on separate rooms and they wouldn't have that at the Manor, not and keep up the fiction that they were blissful newlyweds.

But then again, well, she'd already spent one night in his bed. At least this time she would remember whatever happened there. "All right. I'll stay with you at Maverick Manor."

She got him to drop her off at the boardinghouse and promised to meet him at the Manor in an hour and a half.

Upstairs in her room, Jordyn got right to work packing an overnight bag. Once that was done, she started gathering the rest of her things together for tomorrow. After work she would pile everything into her old Subaru and follow Will out to the ranch.

The door to her room stood ajar as she packed. She'd left it that way on purpose for Melba, who appeared just as Jordyn was tucking a stack of T-shirts into one of the suitcases spread open on the bed.

"So it looks like you're leaving us earlier than you planned," Melba said, huffing a little from the climb up the stairs.

Jordyn went to her. The old woman wrapped her in a hug. Jordyn breathed in her comforting scent. Melba always seemed to smell of lemon polish and cinnamon cookies.

Melba stroked her hair. "I heard the news that you married Cecelia's brother. Congratulations, honey. I know you'll be very happy."

Jordyn felt a sharp stab of guilt at deceiving Melba, who had always been kind and generous to her. "Thank you. I've known Will forever. He's a wonderful man." She stepped back from the old woman's embrace. "I'm sorry I didn't tell you yesterday. It was all kind of sudden."

"Sometimes love is like that."

"Uh, yeah. Yeah, it is—and listen, I'll come back to-morrow, after work, to pick up everything and turn in my key, if that's okay." Melba took her hand and pressed a small piece of paper into it. It was a check, the amount Jordyn had paid ahead for her July rent, plus her original deposit. "Oh, no. Melba, I didn't even give you notice."

"Shh, now." Melba patted her cheek. "Consider it a wedding present from Old Gene and me—and don't you dare be a stranger, you hear? You come back and see me now and then. I want to know all about how married life is treating you."

"I will definitely be back to visit." Until August, anyway, when she would be leaving for good.

Melba gave a pleased little laugh. "And didn't I tell you to have faith, that the perfect man for you would come along?"

More than once in the past two years, Jordyn had cried on Melba's kindly shoulder because everybody else was coupling up and getting married, but she'd yet to meet the guy for her. "Yes, you did."

"And just look at you now."

Jordyn put on a big, fat smile. "You're right. It all worked out in the end." And it had. Just not in the way that Melba assumed. Jordyn *was* married, as she'd dreamed of being. But by the third week in August, barring the slim chance that she might be pregnant, she would be divorced.

Also, when she'd dreamed of marriage, what she'd really been longing for was that special, special man and true love to last a lifetime.

Will was special, all right. And he loved her—as an honorary baby sister he felt he had to take care of.

It was a long, long way from what she'd been dreaming of.

* * *

When she knocked on Will's door at the Manor, he answered with his cell phone at his ear.

He ushered her in and went on with his conversation—with his mother, Carol. "Yeah, Mom. I know. I should have called. Sorry. It is a big, big deal, and I know you hate being left out of the loop...Yeah. Absolutely. You had a right to be here. It's just that, well, when I swept Jordyn Leigh off her feet, I needed to make her mine before she came down to earth and had second thoughts." He glanced Jordyn's way, arching a dark eyebrow and grinning, as if to say, *Boy, do I know how to make this crap up.* And he did. He went on, "I wanted that ring on her finger before she had a chance to think twice. Couldn't have her changing her mind on me, now, could I?" His mother said something and he replied, "Tomorrow, that's right. We'll be moving in then...Thanks. I will..." And then, "Yeah, she's here..."

Jordyn dropped her overnighter on the floor, scowled at Will for putting her on the spot—and then gave in and took the phone. "Hi, Carol."

"Jordyn Leigh, I am so happy." Will's mom had been crying. She sniffled. "I have to say, I always wondered about you two, always suspected there was more going on between you than any of us realized."

Seriously? "And you were so right," she lied. "Just look at us now." She sent Will another scowl. He put on a big smile and gave her a thumbs-up.

"I have to tell you," Will's mom said in her just-between-us-girls voice. "I was beginning to think Will would never find the right woman and settle down. But now I get it. He was waiting to get to Rust Creek Falls—and you. I just... Words fail me. They do. Your mother and I have always dreamed that someday our families would be joined together. And now it's happened. It's really happened. You're my own daughter now. I only wish we could get up there to see you this summer."

"Well, that would be wonderful…" And awkward. And strange.

"But even if we don't make it to visit before the end of summer, we'll see you here at home for Thanksgiving." They would? "Will says you're off to Missoula at the end of August, but he promised to bring you home to us over your Thanksgiving break. And then you'll both be coming down for Christmas, of course."

"Erm, of course…"

"Oh, sweetie, I can't wait."

Jordyn played her part. She said she couldn't wait, either. And Carol Clifton babbled happily on for another ten minutes.

Finally, she asked for Will again. "I have a few more things I need to tell him, and then his father will want to congratulate him."

Jordyn tossed Will the phone as if it was a scalding hot potato, scooped up her overnighter and made a beeline for the bathroom, which gave her a door to shut on Will as he told more brilliantly detailed lies to his own mother.

Determined not to go back out there until Will had finished his call, Jordyn set her toiletry case on the shelf, ran a comb through her hair and put on some lip gloss. She was just peeking around the door to make sure the coast was clear when her own phone rang. It was her mother, who was crying happy tears just like Will's mother had been.

Jordyn emerged into the main room and dropped to the sofa as Evelyn Cates said how thrilled she was about the marriage. She was also hurt that she hadn't been there to see her youngest daughter say *I do* to the man of her dreams. Jordyn talked to her for fifteen minutes, in the course of which her mom got past her hurt and confessed that she was over the moon at the news.

"I've always favored Will over his brothers," her mother confided in an excited whisper. "Though make no mistake, I do love his brothers, too."

"I know you do, Mom."

"And your father and I are going to see what we can do, see if we can make it up there to the Rust Creek Valley for a visit this summer..."

"It would be so great to see you." *Except for how I'll have to lie straight to your face the whole time that you're here.*

"Well, I can't promise anything. Things are always crazy here at home—and you'll be here in Thunder Canyon for Thanksgiving, anyway, won't you?"

She cast a reproachful glance in Will's direction. "That's the plan."

"Wonderful." Her mother sighed. "Just wonderful. I'm so happy for you—and Will is a lucky, lucky man."

Her father came on the phone next. He told her he loved her and he was proud of her and he thought she'd made a damn fine choice in Will for a husband. "And is he there with you? I would like a word with him."

Jordyn passed Will her phone. He got congratulated by her father and then her mother. Twenty minutes later, they finally said goodbye to the Cates parents.

And five minutes after that, Jordyn's sister Jasmine called. Jazzy had come to Rust Creek Falls with Jordyn, but had found love in no time with the local veterinarian, Brooks Smith.

"I've called twice before this and sent more than one text, too, since I heard the news Sunday morning," Jazzy chided in a wounded tone. "I was getting worried."

Jordyn apologized and settled her down and told all

the right lies. Already they were starting to come way too smoothly, those lies. And that seemed somehow a whole new kind of wrong. Bad enough that she kept lying, even worse that the untruths were starting to rise so easily to her tongue.

After she got rid of Jazzy, she looked up to find her new husband watching her. "I would really love it if I didn't have to tell another lie today." She tossed her phone on the low table and sank to the sofa in the room's small living area.

"Hey." He came to her in long strides, dropping down beside her and throwing an arm across the back of the couch. Faintly, she could smell his aftershave, like saddle soap and spice. He had a scruff of black beard on his fine, square jaw, and his eyes really were beautiful, surrounded by long, black lashes that any girl would envy, his irises light as blue frost in the center, the outer circle rimmed in cobalt. "Don't think of it as lying," he advised in that know-it-all tone he'd been using on her practically since she was in diapers.

"Of course I think of it as lying. It *is* lying."

"Because you're approaching it the wrong way. Strictly speaking, nothing we've told them is untrue."

"Strictly speaking," she shot back, "now you're lying to me, too."

"That's not so."

"Think back, Will. You told your parents that you're bringing me home to Thunder Canyon for Thanksgiving— and at Christmas, too."

A muscle in that square jaw twitched. "It could happen."

"If I'm pregnant, which I'm not."

"It's going to be fine. I promise. We just need to stick with the plan."

"Yeah. Our Divorce Plan," she said sourly, already

thinking of it as requiring capital letters, something huge and looming, dishonest and wrong that she'd somehow let Will convince her was right. "And not only are there all the lies we're telling now. Think about how fun it's going to be having to also explain to everyone we love that it 'didn't work out.'"

He studied her for a long, uncomfortable moment and then asked too quietly, "Do you want to call it off now? If you do, just say so."

She should say yes and she knew it. *Yes, Will. Let's put an end to this craziness now.* But she didn't want to call it off. She wanted...

She didn't know for sure what she wanted. But calling it off wasn't it.

His eyes had a hard light in them. "Are you going to answer my question, Jordyn Leigh?"

"I, um..."

"Answer my question."

"Fine. No, then. I don't want to call it off."

His expression gentled. "What do you say we not borrow trouble?" He caught a lock of her hair and rubbed it slowly between his fingers.

She wrapped her fingers around his wrist. "Don't."

They stared at each other. She was pinching up her mouth at him, and she knew it. His skin was so warm against her palm. She found herself remembering the other night—before it all got so crazy and misty and they did things she could no longer recall.

It had been wonderful, that night. She'd loved being with him. And his kisses had thrilled her, just set her on fire...

She didn't know quite how it had happened, but she was staring at his mouth. So soft, that mouth, especially in contrast to the general hardness of him.

Her stomach chose that moment to rumble. That made him grin.

It also broke the strange spell she'd somehow fallen under. "Don't make me smile." She let go of his wrist and pretended to sulk. "I'm too annoyed with you."

"What you are is hungry. We need to get a decent meal into you."

He was right. She really should eat. "They have room service here, I hope."

He shook his head. "I think we need to get out."

"Maybe you do. Find me a menu. I'll hang around here."

"Jordyn, we can't just hide in the room."

"You're the one who's calling it hiding." At that, he simply stared at her disapprovingly until she began to feel like a bit of a brat. Grudgingly, she confessed, "And I've told enough lies for one day."

He shrugged. "Okay. I can understand that. How about this? I know of a really good Italian place in Kalispell."

"We're going back to Kalispell?" She whined the words and almost winced at the grating sound of her own voice.

"Look at it this way. No one there will ask you any questions, and that means you'll be telling no lies."

Will thought that the afternoon went pretty well, overall.

At the Italian place, they shared an antipasto. He ordered three-meat lasagna and she had veal *piccata*. Jordyn asked for a second basket of bread and cleaned her plate.

When they left the restaurant, she seemed in a much better mood. She asked about the ranch.

He told her about the great views of the mountains and the good water access. "It's just what I always wanted, mostly prime grassland and quality bottom land where I can grow alfalfa. But I've also got a few pretty cottonwood groves and pines higher up. The house, bunkhouse, foreman's cottage and the barn—well, just about all of the buildings—need work. I'll be getting to that, but it's livable in the meantime. I've bought cattle, and they'll be showing up within the week, to get me going on my herd. And I've hired a married couple to help out. They'll be coming up from Thunder Canyon, bringing my horses and all the furniture I own, on Thursday or Friday."

"Do I know them?"

"I doubt it. Pia and Myron Stevalik?"

'Nope. Don't think I've met them. You haven't told me what you're going to call the place."

"Shangri-La?"

"Hah. That is so totally *not* you, Will."

"How about the Flying C?"

At that, she nodded. "I like it." And then she sent him a smile.

He felt pleased—with himself, with the sunny afternoon outside the quad cab, with just about everything. "That settles it, then. I'm calling it the Flying C."

She bent and got something from her purse—an elastic band, he saw a moment later, when he glanced her way again. With her gaze on the road ahead, she put her hair up in a ponytail. The action lifted her small, firm breasts even higher.

About then, he realized he was staring. Before she could catch him at it, he faced front again and told himself to quit drooling over her and drive the damn truck.

She said, "So tell me your secret. How'd you get your ranch so soon? I remember when you used to talk about it back home, you always said you hoped that you might swing it by the time you were in your forties." Apparently, she had no clue he'd been staring at her breasts.

Good. "Yeah. That was the plan. But maybe you remember my great-aunt Wilhelmina?"

"Of course. You were named after her, right? And she made it big in real estate in San Diego…"

"That's Aunt Willie. About six months ago, she passed on."

"Oh, Will. I'm so sorry. I hadn't heard." She reached across the console and gave his shoulder a light squeeze then quickly retreated to her side of the cab again. He wouldn't have minded at all if she'd held on for a moment or two longer. The impression of her soft hand seemed to linger through the fabric of his shirt. "How old was she?"

"In her eighties, and she'd been frail for a couple of years. It happened peacefully."

"I'm glad for that."

"She went to sleep one night and never woke up. Aunt Willie had married five times, but never had any children."

"And she doted on you…"

"She was the greatest. I miss her. She left me a generous nest egg and a final letter that told me to 'live my dream' and 'follow my heart.'" He sent her a grin.

"Oh, I like that." Jordyn's eyes got that shine to them. She was a pretty woman. But that shine in her eyes made her downright beautiful. "Your aunt Willie was a romantic."

He chuckled. "To you, everyone's a romantic." They passed the Manor. He didn't turn in.

And Jordyn's eyes went from shining to guarded. "What's up, Will?"

He kept his tone casual. "I just thought we'd go on into town for a little, take a walk in the park."

She was pinching up her mouth again. "I told you. I've done enough lying for one day."

"If we see anyone, we'll just smile, say thank-you when they congratulate us—and walk on by."

She muttered something unpleasant under her breath. He had the good sense not to ask her to say that again.

Will stopped his quad cab in the lot between the park and the veterinary clinic. It was the same lot where Jordyn vaguely remembered Elbert Lutello pulling a briefcase from his pink Cadillac on Saturday night.

Jordyn tried again to get through to her temporary husband. "I don't feel like a walk right now, Will."

"It'll be good for you, a little fresh air, some exercise." He said it so cheerfully, as though he had nothing more on his mind than a late-afternoon stroll.

Bull. "I've known you all my life. You think I can't tell when you're playing me?"

He turned off the engine and adjusted his straw Stetson on his handsome head. "Okay, Jordyn. The truth is I was kind of hoping that a walk in the park might jog loose a few memories of what happened Saturday night."

"But we already know the main points of what happened in the park. The mystery is how we got to your hotel room and what we did once we were in there."

"I admit I don't remember what we did when we got there, but I know we drove there in this pickup." He tapped the steering wheel for emphasis. "That's easy to figure out because I left the pickup here in this lot for the wedding and the party—and the next morning, it was at the Manor."

"Listen to yourself. *That* is scary. We're lucky we made it to the hotel that night without ending up in a wreck."

"Exactly. Another reason that whoever drugged us needs to be called to account for it."

"That's assuming we were drugged in the first place."

"Jordyn, would you just walk in the park with me? Please?" He said it so nicely.

She knew she was weakening. She grumbled, "Anyone

ever tell you that you're like a dog with a bone once you get fixated on something?"

He tugged on the brim of his hat again. "Humor me?"

She cast a glance toward the headliner and puffed out her cheeks with a hard breath. "Oh, fine."

He rewarded her for giving in with a slow, way-too-sexy grin. "You're the best wife I ever had, you know that?"

"You silver-tongued devil, you." She shoved open her door and climbed down to the blacktop. He went around the rear of the truck to meet her. When she started off toward the park, he caught her hand and twined his fingers with hers. She slanted him a wary look.

"We're newlyweds, remember? Newlyweds should hold hands." His hat shadowed his eyes, and she couldn't really read his expression.

But hey. It felt good, his big, warm hand all wrapped around hers. As if she wasn't alone. As if...they really *were* married. Or at least, intimate. Close...

Better not to overthink it. She squeezed his fingers. "Let's go."

They set off. "I think we should start at the beginning," he said, "at that spot by the gazebo, where they set up the punch table and the portable dance floor."

A half an hour later, they'd strolled through most of the small park hand in hand, stopping at any spot either of them could recall from Saturday night. They'd waved and smiled and said hi to a couple of young mothers and some kids tossing a ball.

And neither of them had remembered anything new from the night in question.

"Well, it was worth a shot," Will said as they started across the parking lot on their way back to the quad cab.

"If you say so." They were still holding hands. She

slanted him a smile. "And the walk actually turned out to be kind of nice."

"I knew you'd enjoy it."

"Don't get smug, Clifton."

"I am never smug."

"Yeah, right."

He tugged on her hand, pulling her closer. "And see? No one asked you a single question."

She beamed wider. "True. It was fine."

"Told you so." He tipped his head down to her.

They stopped walking and just stood there, on the edge of the blacktop, grinning at each other. She caught herself on the verge of going on tiptoe to press her lips to his.

Oh, a girl could get so confused in a situation like this. Married for the world to see, both of them playing their parts.

Maybe too well.

Gently, and much too regretfully, she pulled her hand free of his. "I, um, have some homework I should get busy on…"

He frowned, puzzled at first. But then he remembered. "Right. Those online classes you've been taking." He took off his hat, smoothed his black hair and slid the hat back in place. "So. Back to the Manor?"

"That would be great. I'll get out my laptop and get to work."

Will seemed kind of quiet on the drive to the hotel. But then, Jordyn was quiet, too, thinking about how she'd almost tried to kiss him, about how she had to watch herself with him.

That walk in the park had failed to spark any lost memories from Saturday night. But lost memories weren't the only kind. What about the things she *hadn't* forgotten from Saturday night?

Like for instance, Will's kiss. Ironic? Oh, yeah. She couldn't recall if she'd had sex with him or not. But kissing him? She remembered that just fine. And she might as well be honest with herself. She wouldn't mind at all if he kissed her again.

However, given their situation, kissing Will probably fell directly into the "things *not* to do" category. Their situation was plenty complicated already. No need to make it more so.

At the Manor, he walked her to the room and then went off to find his brothers, suggesting she order up room service if she got hungry and promising to be back by ten or so. That gave her four hours on her own. She got out her laptop and went to work.

Once she'd caught up with her assignments, she grabbed a quick shower and put on a comfy pair of terry-cloth shorts and a Grizzlies T-shirt suitable for sitting around in—and sleeping in, when the time came. She had a chicken sandwich and a soda then brushed her teeth and stretched out on the bed to watch a little TV.

The next thing she knew, she heard the shower running. She opened her eyes to the end of a *Scandal* rerun and realized that Will must have come in while she was sleeping.

She switched off the TV and sat up against the pillows and wondered why her heart had started racing a thousand miles a minute. There was nothing to get all excited about. Yeah, it was weird, her and Will in one room with one bed.

But come on. They'd already spent a night together, even if she couldn't remember a thing about what had happened when they did. He was…just Will. They'd known each other forever, and it was not a big deal.

Eventually the shower stopped. She sat there staring

at the bathroom door, ordering her silly heart to slow the heck down.

He came out on a cloud of steam, wearing sweats and a soft gray T-shirt that clung to the hard muscles of his chest and outlined those corrugated abs of his. His feet were bare, and his hair was wet, and her mouth was suddenly desert dry. "Sorry," he said. "I didn't mean to wake you up."

"Oh! You didn't. I was...I didn't mean to fall asleep." Lame. Utterly, completely lame. If she *wasn't* a virgin, she certainly sounded like one—a virgin from way back in the day, one who knew nothing about sex or pleasure or what to do with a man in her room.

Well, she did know. She'd read plenty of books about pleasing her special guy—as well as herself. She was ready and then some for whenever *he* finally bothered to come along.

True, she lacked experience at being intimate with a man and she would be counting on her special guy to help her with that. But she wasn't afraid of her own desires. She was a healthy, normal grown woman who took care of herself in every way, including sexually.

He studied her for a moment. "You okay, Jordyn?"

"Sure. Fine. I mean, all things considered."

His mouth quirked at the corners. "Tell you what. Just give me a pillow. I'll take the couch, and you can turn off the light."

That wasn't right. "No." It kind of popped out without her actually planning to say it. "I mean, come on. It's a big bed, and we've already spent one night together in it."

"I'm taking the sofa."

"But it's too short for you, hardly more than a love seat, really. You won't be comfortable on that."

He had that look, the one she'd always thought of as his

noble look. When she was younger and he got that look, it always meant he was about to start telling her what to do. But now that noble look seemed more directed at himself. He said grimly, "I promised you separate rooms. Tomorrow we'll have them. Tonight the couch will do me fine."

She folded her arms across her breasts and executed a serious eye roll. "This is ridiculous."

"It's not right that you should have to—"

"Shush," she commanded. He surprised her and actually shut up. She wasted no time jumping from the bed, pulling back the covers and climbing in. "There's a blanket in the closet. Grab that. You can sleep outside the covers. I promise not to try and put a move on you."

He chuckled at that and then looked at her sideways. "You sure?"

"Absolutely. Come to bed."

Chapter Five

Will was stretched out beside her in the dark.

She could smell him—all clean and masculine and freshly showered. She stared at the shadows up near the ceiling and wondered if she would ever get back to sleep.

"Jordyn Leigh?" His voice kind of filled up the darkness, so deep and manly and just rough enough to make her wish...

Well, never mind about what she might wish. "Yeah?"

"What's the matter?"

She should tell him there was nothing. But suddenly she felt so safe in the dark, in the bed, with Will. She wanted to share her thoughts, to tell him the thing that kept preying on her mind. "It's just too strange, that's all."

When she said no more, he gently prompted, "What's strange? Tell me."

"Well, I mean, to wait all these years for that special night. And then, not to know if it happened or not."

"It really gets to you, huh?" His voice just wrapped around her, soothing and comforting and wonderfully deep.

She let out a sigh into the darkness. "Yeah, it gets to me."

"You could go to a doctor, get an exam, find out for sure?"

"But see, that's just it…"

A silence. She matched her breathing to his. And then he encouraged her in a near whisper, "Come on. You can tell me."

She thought what a great guy he was. All those years she'd found him so annoying. How wrong she'd been. She confessed, "I looked it up online yesterday while I was trying to get my mind around the whole idea that I can't even remember if we did or we didn't."

"Looked what up, exactly?"

"You know, about hymens."

Another silence from him. He didn't even breathe. She suspected he might be trying not to laugh.

And strangely enough, that he might be holding back a chuckle didn't bother her. Why wouldn't he chuckle over the idea of her madly searching the web for the scoop on her possibly lost virginity? It *was* kind of funny, she supposed.

Just not to her.

Finally, he asked, "Hymens, huh?"

"Mmm-hmm. Turns out they're something of a myth."

"Wait. You're trying to tell me there's no such thing as a hymen?"

"No. They do exist."

"Whew." His voice was teasing now. She smiled to herself in response to the sound of it. "Had me worried there for a minute."

"The thing is some women hardly have one, even when they're really young. And it can get thin and slowly disappear if a woman is an athlete, thus the old wives' tale that women should ride sidesaddle to preserve the proof of their virginity. And by my age, even if a woman's never had sex, she very well might not have much of one left, anyway—and also, a woman can actually have sex and her hymen can stretch, but still be there. So it's a problem, because whether or not I have one wouldn't necessarily tell a doctor anything, unless there was scarring or bleeding or some kind of injury. I don't feel as though I've been injured. And Sunday morning, there was no blood, and I wasn't the least bit sore."

She stared into the darkness, waiting for him to say something else. But he didn't.

So she finished in a small, sad voice, "The plain fact is the most reliable way to find out if a woman's a virgin is to ask her—unless she got drunk off her ass and can't remember, that is."

She waited again, hoping for a few more words of support and comfort from him. But he remained totally silent beside her.

Had he dropped off to sleep?

Not that she'd blame him if he had. What guy wanted to lie in the dark with his clothes on next to his wife who wasn't *really* his wife and listen to her babble endlessly about hymens?

"TMI, huh?" she asked in a trembling whisper.

And that was when she felt his hand, down between them, next to hers. His warm fingers brushed her cool ones. She gave him her hand. He twined their fingers together and lifted their joined hands toward his face. She felt his breath across her knuckles, followed by the soft brush of his lips on her skin.

Jordyn let out the breath she hadn't realized she was holding. Her eyes drifted shut. She fell asleep thinking that as temporary husbands went, she could have done a whole lot worse.

* * *

She woke to daylight and the smell of fresh coffee.

"Mornin'." Will was already up, sitting on the sofa, eating eggs delivered from room service. He indicated a still-covered dish on the tray on the coffee table. "I ordered you the breakfast scramble, wheat toast. Hope that'll work."

She sat up and stretched. "Perfect."

He gave her a look that made her empty tummy feel warm. "Come on, then. Dig in before it gets cold."

So they ate, sitting side by side on the sofa.

After breakfast, he let her hog the bathroom. She had to hurry to get ready for work.

He followed her to the door and pulled it open for her as she juggled her purse and her laptop. "What time will you be through for the day?"

"About three."

"I'll meet you there. We can go by the boardinghouse and get your things. Then you can follow me out to the ranch."

"You don't have to—"

He waved away her objections. "Three o'clock. I'll be there."

She clutched her laptop to her chest. "Wow. Today's the day, huh?"

He looked so pleased with himself. "Closing is at ten."

"Allow me to congratulate you again on the total fabulousness of having your own place at last."

He gave a modest little snort. "I'll be knee-deep in cow crap before you know it."

"But it will be your *own* cow crap." She moved past the threshold into the hallway, but she was leaning up toward him.

And he leaned down to her, his eyes alight with excitement at what the day would bring. "I like a woman who understands the dreams of a ranching man."

She waited for him to kiss her.

And then she realized she was doing it and quickly stepped back. "Well, see you at three, then."

"Three. Right. See you then."

She whirled and headed off down the hall, feeling the heat flooding her cheeks, hoping she'd turned away in time, before he saw her blush.

Will stood in the doorway, staring after Jordyn's excellent backside as she hurried away from him.

He'd almost kissed her.

And from the wide, welcome look in her eyes and the softness of that tempting mouth of hers, he guessed that she would have let him do it. He wished he had, even though the side of him that had always looked out for her wanted to punch his lights out for having such thoughts.

Which made zero sense. He'd kissed her Saturday night, and more than once. He'd likely done *more* than just kiss her. The horse had left the barn for him and Jordyn, kissingwise.

And besides, they were married. Why shouldn't they kiss?

Don't go there, you idiot. Keep yourself in line.

He pulled his head back into the room and shut the door and told himself he wouldn't think about sharing kisses with his adorable accidental wife. It should be easier to keep his hands and his mouth to himself after today. At the ranch, they would have separate bedrooms.

Not like last night, when he'd lain beside her in the dark and listened to her breathing even out into sleep and tried to block out the softness of her body, the sweet scent of her skin—all of her, right there beside him.

And this morning? He woke up spooning her, sporting wood. Lucky for him, she was still asleep. He'd managed to ease himself away from her, slide out of the bed and make it to the bathroom without her waking up and discovering how very happy he was to have her around. It could have been damned embarrassing.

But then again, he *was* a man. Morning wood happened. No big deal.

And anyway, today he would take possession of his ranch. He'd have his room, and she'd have hers.

Problem solved.

"Don't you dare peek, Miss Jordyn," said little Sophie Lundergren.

It was half past noon. They'd all just finished their sack lunches. Sophie sat beside Jordyn at the long picnic table under the giant oak in the play yard at Country Kids Day Care.

"I'm not peeking, I promise," Jordyn vowed, and kept her hands on the tabletop, away from the blindfold Sophie's older sister, Delilah, had tied around her head moments before.

There were giggles from the kids all around her.

And lots of whispering. Someone brushed by her and set something on the table.

One of the boys said, "Shh. Hurry."

And one of her bosses, either Sara or Suzie—she couldn't be sure which—said, "Careful, now. Yes…"

And then, finally, Sara's oldest daughter, Lindy, said, "Ahem. We're ready. Remove the blindfold."

Quick hands untied the bandanna wrapped around Jordyn's head and whipped it away.

And everyone, kids and Sara and Suzie together, cried, "We love you, Miss Jordyn!"

Jordyn blinked and stared—at the leaning stack of brightly wrapped packages piled on one end of the table, at the obviously homemade cake with "Jordyn and Will" printed in lopsided pink letters on top. "Oh!" she exclaimed, and pressed her hands to her mouth. "Oh, my!"

"It's a wedding shower!" exclaimed nine-year-old Lily Franklin. "We're giving you a wedding shower!"

"Yeah!" said Bobby Neworth, who was almost eight. "Because all that lovey-dovey stuff is kind of icky, but cake and presents are good!" The other boys hooted and whistled in noisy agreement.

Jordyn gulped down the huge knot of mixed emotions that had suddenly formed high up in her chest and told herself not to think about the lies, to put her focus on the total sweetness of the moment. "Oh, this is beautiful. Thank you. Thank you, all."

"You're welcome, Miss Jordyn," the kids said, again pretty much in unison.

Lily proudly announced, "We baked the cake yesterday. It's called red velvet. And the frosting is buttercream."

"I did the frosting letters!" Bobby declared. "And Mrs. Suzie only had to help me a teeny-tiny bit."

Jordyn nodded in appreciation. "It looks so good."

"It's a little bit crooked," Delilah allowed.

"It's the best cake I ever had," declared Jordyn, and everybody beamed.

"And we made all the presents, too!" chimed in six-year-old Theodore Brickman.

"You're gonna love them," Sophie decreed.

"Oh, I know that I will." Across the table, Suzie and Sara stood side by side grinning. Jordyn mouthed a teary-eyed *thank you* at both of them and tried not to think how much she would miss them when she left for Missoula.

"Our pleasure," said Sara, pressing a kiss to the plump

cheek of the beautiful eight-month-old baby cradled in her arms. The baby, Bekka Wyatt, was Melba Strickland's great-granddaughter and a new addition as of yesterday to the Country Kids roster.

Delilah turned suddenly wide eyes to Jordyn. "Miss Jordyn, are you *Mrs.* Jordyn now?"

"She certainly is," Sara answered for her.

And all the kids chimed in with, "Mrs. Jordyn."

"Mrs. Jordyn!"

"She's Mrs. Jordyn now!"

Suzie laughed. "So, *Mrs.* Jordyn. Time to cut the cake."

A happy chorus of agreement followed that suggestion. "Yeah!"

"Cake!"

"Cut the cake, Mrs. Jordyn."

"Cut the cake *now*!"

So Jordyn made the first slice and then Suzie took over, cutting kid-sized slices and passing them around. Jordyn got to work opening her presents.

The kids had done well. Each gift was an art project, and each one delighted her. She admired a watercolor of a stick-figure bride and groom holding hands on a patch of green beneath a bright yellow sun. Another present consisted of bits of yellow crepe paper and white lace glued to a paper plate, with a red-lipped, blue-eyed face drawn in the center. "That's you, Miss—er, *Mrs.* Jordyn—the bride," Sophie explained. "See?" She caressed the lace with her little hand. "It's your wedding veil."

Jordyn put her arm around Sophie and gave her a quick hug. "How beautiful. Thank you, Sophie."

"You're welcome," Sophie shyly replied.

There were construction-paper hearts decorated with rickrack and lace, creations in clay molded to form flowers and butterflies, any number of glittery caterpillars made of egg cartons with pipe-cleaner antennae, plus several bright and cheerful finger paintings of nothing recognizable. Jordyn admired each one and thanked each child, after which she had her cake, which was really quite delicious.

They all pitched in to clean up. The kids got a half hour to work off steam on the playground equipment and then they filed inside for story time. Next, there would be naps for the younger ones and a quiet period for the older children.

Once they went in, Jordyn left Suzie and Sara with the children and went to the office at the front of the house. It was Sara's house. They'd added on rooms to either side in front to accommodate the growing day care. It was a great old house, comfortable and sprawling. Jordyn enjoyed working there.

She loved dealing with the kids, but she also found satisfaction in developing new projects for the day care's curriculum. She helped keep the accounts, and she wrote a mean grant application. Suzie and Sara both claimed they didn't know how they'd ever gotten along without her. A few months before, when Jordyn had told them she planned to head for Missoula in the fall, they'd been supportive of her plans for her future, but unhappy at the prospect of losing her. Jordyn hated to leave them. Yes, she wanted a new start. But the twins were a joy to work for—and the kids were the best.

Jordyn opened up the accounting software and then just stared at the screen for a few minutes, torn between getting all choked up with guilty emotion and a big, fat grin. A wedding shower, so beautifully and lovingly planned and executed off-the-cuff yesterday, while she was away for her "honeymoon" day.

Only at Country Kids...

She heard a light tap on the open French doors behind her. "Excuse me?" said a woman's voice. "Jordyn Leigh?"

Jordyn swiveled her chair to find Claire Strickland Wyatt standing in the entry hall behind her. Claire, who always looked beautiful and pulled together with her long hair just so, was baby Bekka's mom, and Melba Strickland's granddaughter. Claire and her family lived in Bozeman, but now and then she and her husband, Levi, would bring the baby to town and stay with her grandparents at the boardinghouse. They'd arrived last Friday, as a matter of fact, for the wedding and the Fourth of July weekend. "Claire! I heard this morning that you were still in town."

Claire gestured vaguely toward the front door. "Sara told me to just come right in during day-care hours…"

"Perfect. Suzie said you'd signed Bekka up with us. She's been a little darling, seems to be settling right in— in case you were wondering."

Claire's gaze slid away. And then she seemed to catch herself. She met Jordyn's eyes again with a brittle smile. "Well, I, um, decided that Bekka and I would stay in Rust Creek Falls for a little while. Levi went on back home. It's work, you know." Claire let out a sad little chuckle. "He's always got work he has to get back for."

By then, Jordyn had no doubt that something was off with Claire. Way off. Undecided whether to mind her own business or ask Melba's granddaughter if something was bothering her, Jordyn volunteered lamely, "I hear you."

Claire's smile seemed stretched to the breaking point. "They needed him at the store."

"Nice for you, though, to get away for a while."

"Oh, it is, yes. Just great. To get away…"

Ugh. Maybe Claire had read that gossip column in the *Gazette* and couldn't make up her mind if she ought to congratulate Jordyn—or offer her condolences.

And whatever Claire might think about Jordyn getting married out of the blue, something else was going on with Melba's granddaughter. Jordyn felt awful for her. She looked totally miserable.

"So, did you hear my big news?" Jordyn went for lighthearted, with a touch of humor, and thought she succeeded pretty well. "Jenny and Braden weren't the only ones who got married on Saturday."

Claire gulped—and then pasted on another uncomfortable smile. "Yes! I did hear. Congratulations. I...don't think I've met him. I..." She seemed to run out of words.

Jordyn offered, "His name is Will Clifton. I've known him forever. He's from Thunder Canyon, like me. We grew up together."

"Ah. Well, Will Clifton is a lucky, lucky man. I hope you'll be very happy together."

"Oh, we definitely will," Jordyn assured Claire with a blithe wave of her hand. What was another lie—or ten— anyway? "It was sudden, our marriage, but so what? I don't care what they say about marrying in haste, sometimes you just know when the right man comes along."

"Of course you do," Claire replied with real feeling. Jordyn dared to think they were getting past whatever awkwardness had charged the air a moment before.

And then Claire burst into tears.

For an awful string of endless seconds, Jordyn just sat and gaped at her.

Claire slapped her hands to her mouth. "Oh, God. I'm so sorry. I don't know what's—" the words caught on a sob "—come over me..." The tears ran down her cheeks and trickled through her fingers.

Jordyn finally stopped gaping and lurched into action. She grabbed the tissue box from the corner of the desk and jumped from her chair. "Claire. Oh, honey..."

"I'm such a complete, hopeless fool…"

"No. No, you are not. Not in the least," Jordyn insisted. "Now, come on. Come and sit down." She passed the other woman the tissue box. Claire took it and clutched it to her chest like a lifeline. Jordyn wrapped an arm around her and guided her over to the love seat opposite the desk. "Sit right here…"

Still sobbing, Claire dropped to the cushions, whipped out a few tissues and dabbed unhappily at her streaming cheeks. "I'll have my mascara all over the place. And you know what? Right this minute, I don't even care."

"Don't worry about your makeup. You just cry."

"It's so embarrassing…"

"No. It's how you feel, and that is never embarrassing." Jordyn sat beside her and patted her shoulder.

"Would you mind if we shut the doors?"

"Not in the least." Jordyn rose again and went over to close and latch the doors. Anyone in the hall could still see them through the glass panes, but the sounds of poor Claire's distress would be mostly muffled.

"I'm so sorry," Claire insisted again. "I don't know what's the matter with me…"

"Shh, now." Jordyn went back and sat with her. "It's okay. It's only you and me. Whatever it is, you just cry it out." Jordyn sympathized with Melba's granddaughter. She'd been there herself on Sunday morning, when she sobbed her heart out over her possibly lost virginity while Will tried to tell her that somehow, the night before, she'd become his wife. "Sometimes it's just all you can do, you know? Sometimes you need that, to let go and let it out."

Claire took a fresh tissue and blew her nose. "I can't believe I'm doing this. You shouldn't have to deal with this…"

"It's okay. Really. I do understand."

Claire dabbed at her eyes. "It was when you mentioned getting married in haste. I, well, the tears just came, and I couldn't stop them."

"Is this about your marriage?" Jordyn dared to ask. "Are you saying that you think you and Levi got married too soon?"

"No." Claire swiped at her wet cheeks. "We didn't rush. We dated for two years before we got married."

"So then what is it? What's got you hurting like this?"

"I don't know, Jordyn." Another hard sob escaped her and she shook her head, hard. "No. That's not true. I *do* know why I'm crying. I know why, exactly."

Jordyn cleared her throat and guessed, "This *is* about Levi, right?"

"Oh, yeah. Levi. Jordyn, I knew the day I met him that he was the one. I knew we would live happily ever after."

The born romantic in Jordyn just had to chime in on that. "Oh, that is beautiful, Claire. I believe in that, I do. In happily-ever-afters. In love at first sight."

"Sometimes," Claire said glumly, "happily-ever-after isn't all it's cracked up to be."

"I'm so sorry…"

"I thought I knew it all, Jordyn. I thought I had love and forever all figured out. But now, well, I have to face the cold, hard truth. I *don't* know. I had it wrong, messed it up. I don't even know how to *talk* to him anymore. The issues keep piling up, and I don't know how to address them."

Jordyn reassured her, "It happens. And I'm sure all married couples have issues." Look at her and Will. They had issues. Like the fact that they'd never planned to get married in the first place, for starters.

"Yes, yes." Claire bobbed her head. "I know you're right. But see, I thought we were better than that, Levi and me. I thought we would get through the tough times, get through the challenges that come with a new baby, get through the loneliness I've been feeling with Levi working all the time. I thought we were managing. But then, Saturday night, after the wedding, I had to get back to Grandma's to relieve the sitter."

"Of course you did."

"I had to get back, and Levi wanted to stay. He was having a good time, he said, and he'd be home soon. For once, couldn't I just let him enjoy himself?"

"That was a little harsh of him."

"I thought so, too. I was hurt. I just turned around and left him without another word. I went back to the boardinghouse, relieved the sitter. And waited. I waited and waited. He'd *said* he'd be home soon. But no. He didn't come staggering in until dawn. And then he tried to tell me he'd hardly had a thing to drink. I mean, what is it Judge Judy says? 'Don't pee on my leg and tell me it's raining?'"

Jordyn couldn't hold back a chuckle. "That Judge Judy, she tells it to them straight."

"Yes, she does. And so did I. I said I knew he was lying. He said no, he wasn't. He didn't even have the integrity to tell me the truth. Well, I wasn't about to stand there and take it while he lied in my face. I said a few things I shouldn't have. And it all went downhill from there. We had a big fight. And…" She paused to blow her nose again. "He *left* me, Jordyn."

"Oh, no…"

"Yes. He did. He left me—well, sort of."

"Sort of?"

Claire drew back her shoulders and aimed her chin high. "Well, all right. I kicked him out. I yelled at him that I didn't want to be married anymore. I yelled at him and kicked him out—and he went. He went back to Bozeman." The waterworks started again. Claire swayed toward Jordyn.

Jordyn gathered her close. "It's okay. You know that." She patted Claire's back. "Just cry…" She stroked Claire's hair and made sympathetic noises as Claire let it all out.

Finally, her sobs faded to sniffles, and Claire straightened from Jordyn's arms. "I simply can't believe he got so drunk. Levi *never* gets drunk."

"I think a lot of people got drunk that night." *Yours truly, among them.*

"He swore up and down that he'd only had a few glasses of punch. I didn't believe him, and I told him so in no uncertain terms. I mean, please. That would be insane, for Braden and Jenny to spike the punch and get everybody falling-down drunk for their wedding reception. Where's the sense in that?"

"There's none," Jordyn agreed, thinking about Will. He was so sure that a certain cowboy had spiked *her* punch. But what if someone had put something right in the punch bowl itself? A lot of people had behaved way out of character that night. Bizarre things had happened. Maybe that punch was at least partly to blame.

Or maybe not. Maybe it was just a case of people kicking over the traces, letting loose and getting crazy on a beautiful summer's night.

Claire heaved a shaky sigh, smoothed a hand down her long sable hair and slowly shook her head. "I can't believe I just unloaded all over you."

Jordyn patted her hand. "It's okay. Believe me, I get it. Sometimes you just need a good cry."

Claire pressed her fingers under her tear-puffy eyes. "I look terrible, don't I?"

"No, you don't. You look like a woman who needed to get something difficult off her chest."

Claire actually smiled then, a trembling smile, but a sincere one. "Grandma adores you. I can see why."

"Aw. I love her right back."

"Do you think I could use the bathroom to freshen up a little?"

Jordyn stood and pulled the doors wide again. "Right this way…" She led Claire to the half bath off the foyer. "I'm guessing you came to pick up Bekka?"

"I did, yes. I'm taking her into Kalispell. Thought I'd do a little shopping, get my mind off my problems."

"Sounds like a great plan. I'll get her for you, why don't I?"

"That would be perfect."

Ten minutes later Claire left with the baby. Jordyn worked on the books for a while then got going on future lesson plans.

At three she got up, went into the entry and peeked out through the sidelight next to the door.

Will was there at the curb in his quad cab, right on time as promised. She smiled at the sight of him. He really was one of the good guys.

She pulled open the door and waved him inside, where she introduced him to Suzie and Sara and the kids. He took it all in stride, answering any and all prying questions, admiring the pile of handmade wedding presents and helping her carry the big box of artistic treasures out to her Subaru.

He put the box in the back, closed the hatch and asked, "So what are you going to do with all those clay butterflies and egg carton caterpillars?"

"I haven't decided yet—maybe decorate my bedroom at the ranch." She grinned at him. "So how *is* the new homestead?"

"The main thing is it's mine." He looked so proud.

"I'm happy for you." She said it softly, with feeling. "Way to go, Will."

He resettled his Stetson, tipping the brim at her. "'Preciate that."

She led the way to the boardinghouse and parked on the street in front. He pulled in behind her.

She started to open her door, but he jogged over and slid into the passenger seat, pulling the door shut behind him. "What?" she asked.

He sent her a guarded glance. "Jordyn…"

"Go ahead. I'm listening."

"I just think I ought to warn you up front that at first, we'll definitely be roughing it. The main house needs work. All the buildings do…"

"Does the roof leak?"

"No."

"Are there lights and heat?"

"Yeah."

"Hot and cold running water?"

"Of course."

"Then we'll manage. And we'll whip it into shape in no time."

For that, he gave her a slow, sexy—and relieved—smile. "You're a good sport, Jordyn Leigh."

A good sport. It wasn't the kind of compliment that made a girl blush with pleasure, but she felt his sincerity, and that warmed her heart. "Come on," she said, and pulled on her door handle. "Let's get my stuff and get moving."

After they'd hauled everything out to the vehicles, Jordyn introduced Will to Melba and Old Gene, and handed over her key.

Old Gene shook Will's hand. "You're a very lucky young man. You take care of this sweet girl, now."

Will played the sincere groom to perfection. "Yes, sir. I certainly will."

Melba tugged Jordyn aside for a last hug. "I do hate to see you leave us…"

Jordyn promised her again to keep in touch. She thought of Claire and whispered, "I saw Claire at Country Kids today. She told me that she and Bekka are staying here with you for a while."

"She told you about her troubles?" At Jordyn's nod, Melba clucked her tongue. "I'm telling myself that she and Levi will work it out."

"I know they will," Jordyn replied with maybe a little more confidence than she felt. It never hurt to keep things positive.

Will said goodbye to Old Gene and ushered Jordyn out the door.

She paused once they were down the porch steps to look back at the old boardinghouse. "It's so weird, walking away this time, knowing I really don't live there anymore…"

He pulled her close to his side, just like a real husband might do. "You going to be all right?"

She took comfort from the warmth and strength of his sheltering arm. "Yeah. I will. I'll be just fine."

He gave her shoulder a squeeze. "Next stop, Crawford's. We need to grab a few things."

She left him to get in her Subaru as he climbed into his truck.

He drove the few blocks to North Main and pulled into the parking lot at Crawford's General Store. They parked side by side, and then got out and stood between the vehicles while he explained what they had to shop for.

"Foodwise, we need the basics. At least enough for tonight and tomorrow morning."

"What about furniture? Will we be sleeping on the floor?"

"There are a couple of old beds left behind by the previous owners, and some dusty-looking mattresses. I saw a beat-up table and some mismatched chairs in the kitchen. The living room is empty. Like I said before, it's pretty sparse."

"Pillows, sheets, blankets, towels?"

"We'll have to buy them—and you know, maybe we ought to just stay at the Manor for another night. Tomorrow I'll head for Kalispell and spend the day getting everything we need to set us up."

"Will."

He eyed her sideways. "You're looking obstinate, Jordyn Leigh."

"You're a Clifton. I'm a Cates. We come from sturdy stock. Crawford's has the basics. Let's get what we can't do without and head for the ranch."

"It's too much to ask. You have to get up early and get to work in the morning."

She knew that he would rather be out at his new place, and she intended that he should have what he wanted. "What did I just tell you, Will?"

He was weakening. "You're sure?"

"Positive. Now let's go."

They walked into Crawford's and right away, Will spotted those two middle-aged ladies from Sunday afternoon. Apparently, the two of them spent a lot of time shopping.

The two caught sight of him and Jordyn and instantly started whispering together.

Will gave them a friendly wave. They nodded and smiled—and went right back to whispering again. About then, it occurred to Will that he and Jordyn needed to play this thing right.

Jordyn pulled a cart free from the row by the doors and wheeled it around toward him. "Let's get the linens and some cleaning supplies first, then we'll get food for tonight and tomorrow." As she came even with him, he reached out, grabbed her fingers from the cart handle and reeled her in close. She made a small, breathless sound, braced her hands on his chest and stared up at him, wide-eyed. "Will! What are you—?"

He bent his head and nuzzled her shining, sweet-smelling hair. "Haven't you noticed?"

"What?"

He rubbed his nose against hers and whispered, "People are watching. And we *did* just get married."

She gave the cutest little sigh. "Oh. Well. I see…"

"Do you?" He tipped up her chin with a finger and settled his mouth gently on hers.

Chapter Six

Jordyn let out a little squeak, a squeak that turned into another soft sigh. And then she slid her hands up and wrapped them around his neck, pressing her slender body close to his. They were a great fit, just right.

And by then, she was kissing him back, stirring vague memories of Saturday night, reminding him that he really liked kissing her. She smelled so good, and she tasted like a ripe peach.

Little Jordyn Leigh Cates. Who knew?

When he lifted his head, he whispered, "We're newlyweds, remember? We're newlyweds who can't keep their hands off each other."

"Ah," she whispered back, her cheeks pink, a soft smile on those plump lips he would be only too happy to kiss every chance he got. "You mean we need to provide a public display of affection for the benefit of anyone who might doubt how very much in love we are?"

"Exactly."

"Or we could just ignore all the gossips and go about our business, not caring in the least what small-minded people might say." She started to pull away.

He caught her arm. Gently. "Jordyn…"

"What?" She gave him one of those challenging looks—the kind she'd been giving since she got out of diapers.

He didn't let that look of hers stop him. "I think you really need to kiss me again."

She giggled, a happy, playful sound. It caused an ache in the center of his chest. A really good ache. And then she scrunched up her eyebrows, pretending to think it over. Finally, she agreed, "Only one more. We have a lot of shopping to do."

"I guess I'd better make it good."

"Yes, you'd better."

So he kissed her again. Not too deep. It was a public place, after all. He made that kiss slow and tender. It wasn't hard—kissing her felt so right.

Too right? Oh, yeah. But now wasn't the time to get all tied in knots because he just possibly might be developing a too-powerful attraction to his childhood friend and temporary bride.

When he lifted his head that time, they shared a knowing smile. And when she pulled away, he didn't stop her—even though he really wouldn't have minded kissing her some more, just standing there by the carts in Crawford's, with Jordyn Leigh in his arms, his mouth pressed to hers.

For maybe a lifetime or so.

The ranch was a beauty, Jordyn thought. Acres of rolling green land, dotted here and there with stands of cottonwood and pine. Fall Mountain, a local landmark, could be seen in the distance, with the snowcapped peaks of the Rockies looming even farther out.

The ranch compound included the main house, the foreman's cottage, a bunkhouse, a barn and corrals, with a series of fenced pastures close in. The stock pond, over a rise not far from the circle of buildings, was fed by a creek, which meandered through the property.

Will stopped to open the driveway gate, and she pulled in behind him. He leaned in her window before he got back in his truck. "Did you see the creek?"

"Yeah."

"Good trout fishing in that creek." He pointed at the gate. "Picture an arch overhead with *Flying C* in wrought iron."

"Sounds perfect."

"But one thing at a time…"

They shared a quick smile. He tapped the side of her door and took off at a jog back to his pickup. They went through the gate and drove on to the circle of buildings. She parked next to him in a bare spot in front of a two-story, white-sided, blue-shuttered farmhouse with a wraparound porch.

"It's charming," she said when he pulled open her door for her.

He made a low, rueful sound. "It will be, in time."

She got out and they went up the weathered steps to the door, which was painted a tired blue and had a fan-shaped window at the top. He had the key in his hand.

The door creaked on its hinges as he pushed it inward onto a foyer, with stairs in the center leading to the upper floor, a bare living room on the left and an empty dining room to the right. He hung his hat on a peg by the door.

"The bones are good," she said. The walls had been whitewashed, and heavy, beautiful old beams crossed the ceilings. The floor was scuffed and dusty, but made of good wide-planked hardwood. The windows were the old-fashioned sash kind.

"Master bedroom's here, with separate bathroom," he said, as they moved deeper into the first floor and passed by it on the left. He took her to the kitchen, which had a battered gate-leg table and three mismatched chairs, wood counters, a great old farm sink, an avocado-green range leftover from the seventies and a refrigerator to match.

She pulled open the fridge. It was working, and it was empty. And wonder of wonders, it was clean. "We can start loading this puppy up right away," she told him happily.

He chuckled. "You are so easy to please."

She met his fine blue eyes. They crinkled at the corners with his wonderful smile. She felt the sudden, lovely echo of his kiss on her lips and had to stop herself from raising a hand and brushing her fingers against her mouth.

This wasn't bad, her and Will, playing at being married. It wasn't bad at all.

In fact, it was really, really fun.

Maybe too much fun...

She could almost feel guilty.

But, hey. Wait a minute. They had a plan, and she intended to follow it through. No reason to beat herself up over the choice she'd made. Might as well make the best of it.

And with Will as her short-term husband, making the best of it wouldn't be all that tough. He was so easy to look at, and he kept a good attitude.

Plus, there were bound to be opportunities for more of those lovely PDAs...

He said, "Let's move along."

And they did. They passed the half bath, which had a cute pedestal sink. She glanced in the utility room. It had an empty space where the washer and dryer should be.

They poked their heads out the back door, and she admired the wide back porch. From there, they returned to the front hall and climbed the stairs.

The second floor offered two bedrooms, a shared bath and a sitting area that overlooked the bare backyard and had a great view of the barn and the creek and the stock pond shining in the afternoon sun.

"Do I get my choice of these two bedrooms up here?" she asked.

He turned from the view out the sitting room windows. "Unless you want the master..." They shared another long look.

She liked that, too, sharing long looks with him, feeling as if they were keeping a really good secret, just between the two of them.

"Forget it," she said. "I'm not kicking you out of your bedroom."

"Whichever one you want, Jordyn, it's yours." His voice had that rumble to it, a rough, manly sound that sent sparks flashing along the surface of her skin. For a long moment, she just stared at him, because it was no hardship, looking at Will.

Wake up, woman. Choose a room. "I'll take the one over the living room. It already has a bed." The bed in question was an ancient cast-iron affair, with a rolled-back mattress braced against the head of it. It didn't look all that comfortable. But at least she wouldn't have to sleep on the floor.

She followed him back downstairs and out to the vehicles.

They unloaded everything. As soon as they had it all inside, they got to work. By a little after seven, they had the kitchen wiped down, the fridge stocked with the basics, the other food put away and the two beds made and ready for bedtime.

Jordyn got to work on dinner, which consisted of ham sandwiches, potato chips, Crawford's amazing dill pickles and cold cans of beer. They were just sitting down to enjoy the feast when Will's cell rang.

Will glanced at the display before answering. "It's Cece. She's called more than once since Sunday, so I'd better answer this time." He took the call.

Jordyn set down her half-finished pickle and listened to him tell his sister the story they'd agreed on. "Yep. That's right, Cece…Uh-huh, we are…I know, I know. It's a surprise, but it's real. Me and Jordyn Leigh are in love and married and damned happy about it." He winked at her across the table.

She forced a smile for him, but she felt a stab of regret that she hadn't called Cecelia before now. They'd been friends forever, she and Cece. Maybe they didn't get together as much as they used to, now that Cece had married Nick Pritchett and they'd moved out of the boardinghouse and into their own place. But still. Jordyn had married Cece's brother, for heaven's sakes. The least Jordyn could have done was pick up the phone and share the news.

Share the lies is more like it…

And really, that was what bothered her, wasn't it?

She might be having a ball, playing house with Will. But she needed to get real with herself, at least. She hadn't called Cece because she hadn't been looking forward to telling her lifelong friend the same lies she'd been telling everyone else.

Lot of good not calling had done. In the end, she would be telling the lies, anyway.

"She's right here," said Will. "Love you, too. Hold on." He offered the phone.

Jordyn took it. "Hey," she said weakly.

"Jordyn. How *are* you? Why didn't you call?" The familiar sound of Cece's voice made her throat clutch.

She gulped to loosen it and got on with the excuses. "I'm fine. Wonderful. And Cece, I know I should have called. It's been total craziness. I hope you'll forgive me for being so thoughtless."

"Oh, stop. There's nothing to forgive. Just as long as you're happy…"

"I am." She gave Will another big, bright smile. "*So* happy. I know, it's sudden. But it's, um, what we both want. Did Will tell you? We're at the ranch now. We moved in just this afternoon."

"I hear it's rustic."

"Yeah, but it's beautiful. I can't think of any place on earth I'd rather be than here at the Flying C with Will." Across the table, her for-the-moment husband nodded his approval.

"Well, then, congratulations to you both."

"Thanks so much, Cece. Love you."

"Love you, too—and we missed you last night."

With a sigh of dismay, Jordyn remembered. "Omygosh. I don't believe it. I missed the Newcomers Club." She and Cece had formed the club a year before to help recent transplants to the community find friends and get involved in their new hometown. Jordyn hadn't missed a meeting all year. "I'm so sorry. It totally slipped my mind."

"Don't beat yourself up over it. It's not a big deal. You *are* a newlywed, after all."

Yeah, but not for long. "I should have been there."

"Oh, come on. There's always next month."

Which would be her *last* month. By the September meeting, she would be settled in Missoula. Why did that make her sad? It was her new life, after all. And she was looking forward to it.

Cece seemed to read the direction of her thoughts. "Are you still running off to Missoula now?"

"I am not *running off* anywhere, thank you very much."

Cece made a humphing sound and Jordyn could just picture her rolling her eyes. "Don't get so sensitive. Let me rephrase. Are you still moving to Missoula to pursue your degree?"

"Yes, my plans are the same. Will won't hear of my backing out on the education I've worked so hard for." Across the table, Will saluted her with his beer can. She puffed out her cheeks and crossed her eyes at him and then went on. "It'll only be for two semesters, and Missoula's just a couple of hours away."

"So you'll be back often," said Cece. "I know I can count on that, now that your husband's here."

Defensiveness curled in her belly. "Now, what is that supposed to mean?"

Cece released a slow, careful breath. "The truth is, I was worried that you'd take off for college and I'd hardly ever see you again. But now that you're married to my brother, I know you have to come home. And that's a very good thing."

Home. Strange how Rust Creek Falls really did feel like home now.

However, when she left for Missoula, she had no plans to return. And by then, she wouldn't be married to Cece's brother anymore...

"Jordyn Leigh," Cece prompted. "Are you still on the line?"

Jordyn shook herself. "I'm right here. I...well, I was just thinking that I don't know how I'm going to bear being away from him. It's going to so *hard*." When she said that, Will put his hand against his heart and mimed frantic beating. She picked up her half-eaten pickle and threatened him with it. He played along and put up both hands in mock surrender. She stuck out her tongue at him, set the pickle back down and said to Cece, "He's one of a kind, your brother."

Cece groaned. "He's a pain in the butt."

Jordyn laughed. "But in a good way—the *best* way."

"Wow, Jordyn Leigh. Look who's changed her tune. He used to drive you crazy."

"Oh, he still does. He really, really does…" She said that with over-the-top breathlessness. Will arched a brow and looked at her sideways. She should have left it at that, but she didn't. She was kind of on a roll. "He's so amazing, Cece. He's so good and kind. And hot looking. And helpful. His kisses just blow me away. And when we're alone, he—"

"Enough," Cece warned. "I know you're in love with him. I get that. But don't give me too many details. He *is* my brother, after all."

Jordyn winced. "Sorry. I think I got carried away…"

Across the table, Will sipped his beer and watched her through suddenly unreadable eyes.

Cece said, "Okay, I'll let you go. I just had to check in, congratulate you both and tell you I love you."

"Thanks. We're fine. Happy. Glad to be here in our new home."

"If you need anything…"

"I will call you if I do, I promise. Love you."

"Bye."

Jordyn turned off the phone and pushed it across to Will. She sipped her beer then picked up the other half of her sandwich. She felt…edgy now, her skin all prickly and hot.

Will leaned back in his chair and stretched a muscular

arm out on the table beside his empty plate. "Wow, Jordyn Leigh. That was…impressive."

All at once, she was totally annoyed with him. "Don't get on me, Will. I'm just doing my best, playing my part."

"Never said you weren't."

She plunked her sandwich back down without taking a bite. "If you've got something you want to say to me, well, you just go ahead and say it."

He turned his beer can in a slow circle on the scarred surface of the old table. "Now you're pissed off at me. Why?"

"*I'm* pissed off? No. Uh-uh. *You* are."

"On the phone with my sister, you sounded way too grown-up. You almost had me convinced that you and I are good and…intimate. But now, three minutes later, you're acting like a ten-year-old."

I hate you, Will Clifton, she thought, but somehow managed not to say. Talk about childish behavior. She drew in a long breath and let it out slowly. "I'm sorry. It's what I said to Cece. I just kind of got carried away. You and me, we're so busy fooling everyone, holding hands, kissing in Crawford's, telling the world how *happy* we are. Sometimes it feels like I'm fooling myself, too."

He stared at her for a long, very uncomfortable string of seconds. Then he shoved his plate aside, leaned toward her and stretched out his hand across the table. His lean fingers beckoned.

She gave him her hand. It felt good to have her hand engulfed in his big, rough, warm one.

Too good.

She ought to pull away.

But she didn't. "Oh, Will. Should we really be doing this? I mean, it's just a big lie."

He scowled. "No, it's not. We *are* married."

"Let's not go through all that again. Please."

"Jordyn, if you're having second thoughts, you need to tell me. We'll deal with them."

"It's only… Sometimes it seems so real, you know, you and me? So natural, so right."

"And that's bad?"

"Well, it does kind of scare me. I get all confused between what's real and what isn't."

He turned her hand over, smoothed her fingers open and drew a slow circle in the center of her palm. Talk about intimate. Her breath tangled in her throat, and a flush stole up her cheeks. She wished he might just keep on doing that for a very long time, keep holding her hand, brushing a sweet circle onto her skin.

And then he said, "This isn't the first time you've acted like you want to call it off."

"Call it off?" she repeated in a stark whisper.

He nodded. "I don't like it, but I can accept that maybe this just isn't something you're willing to do. You can move back to the boardinghouse. We'll tell everyone we realized it wouldn't work, after all. But then, if there's a baby, I want you to promise me that you'll come back."

Call it off…

Did she want that?

They'd been "married" for just three days. Not only did she have to deal with her guilt over the lies they were telling, but sometimes when she told a lie, it came out seeming way too much like the truth.

The stuff she'd just said to Cece, for instance. About how wonderful Will was, how superhot and protective, how when he kissed her, she melted…

Well, she found it easy to tell those lies because those lies felt so very true.

It didn't seem possible. She didn't know how it had happened. But somehow, Will Clifton was beginning to look like her dream man.

And that was scary. That made her wonder if this temporary marriage could turn out to be way more dangerous than she'd realized at first—dangerous to her tender heart.

"Jordyn Leigh," he prompted softly. "Are you ever going to answer my question?"

"Yes. Yes, I am."

"*Do* you want to call it off?"

"No, Will," she confessed in a small voice. "I don't want to call it off. I don't want to move back to the board-inghouse."

He smiled at her then. *Bam!* That smile reached out across the table and wrapped itself around her heart. "All right, then. We're still on."

"Still on," she answered in a voice that only wobbled a little.

"We get along," he reminded her.

She agreed. "Yeah."

"We *like* each other."

She chuckled and gave his fingers a squeeze. "Well, most of the time."

He remained completely serious. "We are married and it's *our* marriage, the way *we* want it, for as long as it lasts."

"Yes, Will."

"We have an agreement."

"We do," she replied solemnly. "And we'll stick to our plan…"

Chapter Seven

Will woke at the crack of dawn the next morning to the sound of a baby crying. The wailing seemed to be coming from the backyard.

"What in the...?" He jumped out of bed, yanked on his jeans and ran for the bedroom door that opened on to the back porch.

Three goats stood at the base of the back steps. One was a gestating doe. She was silent, gazing at him through big, wet, hopeful eyes. Another doe calmly nibbled at a sad-looking bush tucked up close to the steps. The third, a big, bearded billy, stared calmly at Will—and cried like a baby.

Literally. The damn goat sounded just like a wailing infant. And somehow, that critter managed to look damn pleased with himself as he did it.

Jordyn, wearing pink track pants with *Juicy* printed in silver foil across her butt, a Thunder Canyon Resort T-shirt and fat socks, bumped through the door from the kitchen. She gaped at the trio of animals and then groaned, "Goats?"

Will explained, "I think they may have been left by the previous owners. I heard they kept goats. These three probably got loose when they were trying to load them up to haul them away." He grinned at her. She looked so cute in her pink pants and faded T-shirt, with her gold hair all tangled from sleep. "Good morning."

"Mornin'. So will you call the previous owners to come and get them?"

"I will, yes."

"Do you think they'll come?"

"No idea."

The billy kept bawling.

"He's hungry," she said. From the fence by the barn, a rooster suddenly crowed. "And don't tell me. The previous owners kept chickens, too."

"Yep."

"What are we going to feed them?"

"I'll corral the goats and buy them feed today—and I'll get something for that rooster, too, and whatever other chickens might be wandering around."

She wasn't satisfied with that. "But that big one keeps crying. He's hungry *now*—and you know they're vulnerable to predators, just wandering around loose like that."

"I can only do what I can do."

She braced her fists on her hips and gave him one of those disgusted looks she'd been giving him practically since the day she was born. And then she mimicked, faking a deep voice, "*I can only do what I can do. What is that* supposed to mean?"

He just kept on grinning. Even cranky, she really did kind of brighten up the day. "It means they don't appear to be starving. They'll last on whatever they can forage until I feed them. And so far, they've done an okay job of avoiding any animal who might want to eat them."

The billy must have figured out that Jordyn was the soft touch. He turned his knowing eyes on her and wailed all the harder.

"You are a heartless man, Will Clifton." Jordyn went down the steps, her hand outstretched.

"You know you ought not to encourage them."

She sniffed his suggestion away and plunked down on the bottom step. The goats moved in close, butting her hand, nuzzling her shoulder. She petted them and cooed, "Yes, you are nice guys. Will says he'll feed you. You just have to be patient until he gets around to it, because he's a big meanie, oh, yes, he is…"

"Watch out. One of them will eat those pink pants right off you."

She sent him a cool glance over her shoulder. "Go put on a shirt."

Stifling a laugh, he ducked back into his bedroom, where he grabbed a quick shower, put on his work clothes and ambled out to the kitchen. He found Jordyn loading up the coffeepot.

Yesterday at Crawford's he'd bought the minimum to outfit the kitchen, including the coffeemaker, a set of sturdy pottery dishes, basic glassware, some flatware and utensils, two fry pans, three mixing bowls and a cute red toaster.

They whipped up breakfast together—well, she fried the sausage and scrambled the eggs. He set the table and burned the toast.

The billy goat serenaded them with baby wails as they ate, his bleating punctuated several times by the rooster's crowing.

"I'll clean up," he said when she carried her plate and

mug to the sink. "I know you need to get ready and get to town."

She put down her dishes and turned to him. "Is there anything I can pick up at Crawford's on the way back from work? I know you've got an endless list of stuff to buy and things to do."

He shook his head. "I've got it all handled."

She braced her hands on the sink rim behind her and crossed one stocking foot over the other. Her pretty breasts poked at that faded T-shirt, and he had to remind himself not to stare. "You paid for everything yesterday. It was a lot. I saw the bill when Mrs. Crawford rang it up."

"I planned to buy that stuff. It's all in the budget and not a problem."

"It's a huge undertaking, Will, outfitting a ranch."

He realized he'd better make his situation clearer. "That money Aunt Willie left me? It was a lot. Plenty to buy this place and fix it up, build my herd, whatever I need, even a few luxuries if I happen to want them. And I have investments now, believe it or not. With what she left me, plus what I had saved up over the years, I'm doing just fine. You don't need to worry if I can afford the feed for those freeloading goats out there."

China-blue eyes widened. "Really?"

He nodded. "God's honest truth."

"Will Clifton, rich guy," she said in a musing tone.

He looked her up and down, because she was a pure pleasure to look at, with pink in her cheeks and all that mussed-up yellow hair and that plump mouth he liked kissing. A lot. "You treat me right, little lady, and I'll feed your goats for you."

She blinked. "Oh, great. Now they're *my* goats."

"You were the one sitting on the step out there, talking baby talk to them."

She gave him one of her why-do-I-put-up-with-you looks. "I think I'd better go get ready for work."

He watched her go, the silver letters on her shapely butt bouncing with every step—not a lot, just enough to give any red-blooded man ideas. All those years, he'd thought of her as a baby sister, someone he needed to look out for. He'd always known it bugged her no end that he treated her like a kid.

Now, well, he still knew how to give her a bad time. However, he didn't feel brotherly toward her in the least. Protective, yes. But it wasn't the same as before. Not since those first moments by the punch bowl on the Fourth of July, when it hit him like a bolt from the blue that little Jordyn Leigh Cates wasn't so little anymore. Uh-uh. Jordyn Leigh was all grown-up and looking mighty fine.

He might as well be honest with himself, at least. He was having a great time playing newlyweds with Jordyn Leigh.

But he knew he had to watch himself. If there was no baby, she would be gone before September. She had a dream, and she was going to fulfill it.

He wouldn't stand in her way.

But he *did* wish he could remember all of Saturday night. Whatever had actually happened when they got back to Maverick Manor that night, he wanted those memories of her. He wanted to keep them for himself when she was long gone from Rust Creek Falls.

And thinking about Saturday night reminded him. He needed to make time to have a talk with someone at the sheriff's office about his suspicions concerning that unknown cowboy in the white hat.

After Jordyn left for town, Will made some calls—to his Realtor concerning the abandoned goats and chickens, and to the local satellite company, who promised they could be out the next day to get him set up with TV and internet.

Once he'd handled the phone calls, he drove to Kalispell. He visited a grocery store, a feed store and a couple of department stores. By the time he was finished, he had another pickup load of stuff they needed right away at the Flying C. Basic living room furniture, a wide-screen TV and a washer/dryer combo would be delivered first thing in the morning.

He drove back to Rust Creek Falls and stopped in at the sheriff's office, where he talked to a Kalispell detective named Russ Campbell. Campbell, Will learned, filled in at the sheriff's office when Sheriff Gage Christensen needed him.

A few minutes into his interview with the detective, Will realized he had zero real evidence for his suspicion that an unknown cowboy had put something in Jordyn's drink. He'd seen that cowboy once, and all the guy had done was wink at Jordyn. It was hardly proof that the stranger had tampered with her punch.

Plus, Will's best argument that a mind-altering substance had been slipped in the punch was his on-the-fly marriage, which neither he nor Jordyn could clearly recall. Will wanted the detective—and everyone else in town—to believe that his marriage was the real deal. He didn't want to say outright that he and his bride had been in no way a couple before July Fourth.

He did admit that both he and Jordyn had become strangely intoxicated that night and that they'd both suffered serious hangovers the next morning. They'd each downed several cups of punch, yes, but that had been over a seven-hour period. And Jordyn had been reassured by the bride that there wasn't enough alcohol in the punch to get anyone drunk, anyway.

The detective nodded. "That was my understanding, too. The punch contained only a very small amount of sparkling wine."

Will began to wonder if the detective knew more than he was telling. "So you were there that night?"

"That's right." Campbell said he'd been recruited by the sheriff to provide a police presence at the wedding reception—not because anyone expected trouble, but because the venue was a public park. Campbell said he'd seen the way people behaved that night. He reminded Will that lots of folks had gotten wild.

And Will asked, "Are you saying you suspect that someone put something right in the punch bowl?"

"I'm not saying anything," replied the detective. "Not at this point. But I'll talk to Sheriff Christensen about what you've reported. I promise you, we'll check into it."

Will left the sheriff's office with no more answers than he'd had when he went in. But Russ Campbell had definitely seemed interested in why so many people had behaved so strangely that night. Will believed the detective when he said he'd look into it.

He went back to the ranch. Jordyn drove up while he was still unloading his pickup, so she helped him haul the rest of the stuff inside. They put the perishables away together, making fast work of everything.

In the meantime, the goats showed up at the back steps, and the billy started wailing again.

"We *really* need to feed them," Jordyn said.

So they lured the goats into the smallest of the nearby pastures, which was next to the barn and pretty overgrown. They fed them, filled the water trough and left them to graze on the weeds. They also scattered feed in the back-yard for any random chickens.

Jordyn carried the rest of the chicken feed to the barn. Will went inside and opened a beer.

Five minutes later, she bustled back in, washed her hands and grabbed the roasted whole chicken he'd bought at the store for their dinner. She took the bird out of its plastic container, plunked it on the pull-out cutting board, grabbed a big knife and sawed it in half.

"Jordyn?"

"Hmm?" She tossed half the chicken back into the container.

"What are you doing to our dinner?"

She rinsed and dried her hands. "There's a mama cat with five kittens in the barn." She rolled off a long strip of paper towel and scooped up the other half of the chicken in it. "She needs protein to feed that litter."

"If there's a mama cat in the barn," he helpfully explained, "she's supposed to catch mice for her protein."

Jordyn ignored his remark and headed for the door. "I'll pick up some cat food tomorrow on the way home from work," she said as she went out.

Will let her go. She had that look. He knew damn well she would feed that cat no matter what he said to try and talk her out of it. He finished his beer and made a mental note to ask his Realtor if the former owners had left a pregnant cat behind along with the goats and the chickens.

Jordyn came back inside ten minutes later. By then it was after five.

Will made a decision. "It's only a half hour to Kalispell. Let's go there for dinner."

She started in with all the reasons that going out was a bad idea. "It's a waste of money."

"I'm a rich guy, remember?"

"We've got a lot of stuff to put away. And I'm sweaty from wrangling goats."

"The stuff isn't going anywhere. You want a shower, take one. Ten minutes and we're out of here."

"Ten minutes! Are you crazy?"

He suggested, "You'll never make it if you waste your time arguing with me."

Fifteen minutes later they were on their way.

They'd both liked that Italian place where they'd eaten the other day, so they went there again.

As they ate, he told her about his visit with Detective Campbell. "The detective did remind me that a lot of people acted out of character on Saturday night. It got me thinking that maybe your punch wasn't the only punch someone tampered with."

She twirled spaghetti on her fork. "Now you think someone tried to poison the whole town?"

"I don't know what to think—except that maybe I ought to leave this case to law enforcement."

"So now it's a *case*, is it?"

"Campbell's going to be looking into it."

She ate the forkful of spaghetti. "So we've got the law after the nefarious punch poisoner."

"Yes, we do."

"Now we just need to find out whoever writes Rust Creek Ramblings and blow their cover. We can think of it as a public service to the whole town." She pulled garlic bread off the loaf. "Then again, we all love Rust Creek Ramblings…"

He chuckled. "You're right. It's funny and full of heart. We only hate it when one of the columns is about us."

She leaned toward him, eyes alight. "But seriously, Will. Who do you think writes that column?"

"I'm the new guy in town. How would I know?"

"It's someone who's scarily observant, someone who has a way with words. Maybe a teacher, like Willa Traub, the mayor's wife. Or Kristen Dalton. Do you know her?"

"I don't think so…"

"Daughter of Charles and Rita Dalton? Has a twin sister, Kayla?"

"Sorry. Not ringing a bell."

"Well, Kayla's quiet, shy as a mouse. Kristen, though, she's really feisty. She loves acting and she's involved in a little theater here in Kalispell. Kristen never met a party she wouldn't crash. Being a secret gossip columnist is something Kristen might do because she's a rebel at heart."

"How do you know the columnist isn't a guy?"

"You're right." She laughed. "Maybe it's Homer Gilmore."

"Never heard of him."

"He was at the wedding reception Saturday. In his eighties, rarely shaves, has a strange look in his eye?"

Will sipped from his water glass. "Nope. Don't remember him, either."

She playfully wagged a finger at him. "You need to get to know your neighbors."

"Give me time, woman. I've lived here less than a week."

"Homer's actually kind of sweet. He's originally from Whitehorn, came to town last year. I heard they found him wandering in the woods, claiming he was the ghost of Christmas past."

Will grunted. "You're not serious."

"Oh, yes, I am."

"I hope he got help."

"He's fine, really. Just quite a character—and then again, no. I don't think he could be the mystery columnist. Maybe he has literary talents I'm unaware of, but someone was already writing the column when Homer showed up in town." She shook her head. He watched her, thinking how cute she looked, her hair pulled up in a loose pony-tail, twirling another bite of spaghetti.

In fact, he was so busy admiring his temporary bride, he didn't notice the woman approaching their table until she spoke.

"Will? Jordyn Leigh Cates? I don't believe it…"

It was Desiree Fenton from Thunder Canyon, of all people. He and Desiree had dated a couple of years back. It hadn't ended well.

Will put on a smile. "Desiree. This is a surprise." And not really a good one.

Jordyn set down her fork and gave the other woman a little wave. "Hey, Desiree. How've you been?"

Desiree played it perky. "Terrific." But then she frowned in thought. "Wait a minute. I remember now—Jordyn, you moved up here after the flood, didn't you?"

"That's right. Rust Creek Falls needed help with re-construction."

Desiree asked Will, "Didn't your sister move here at the same time?"

He nodded. "They came together, Jordyn and Cece—and Jordyn's sister, Jasmine, too."

Jordyn put in, "We were looking for a fresh start, I guess you could say."

"I heard all about it." Desiree was smiling now, a know-ing sort of smile. "So many Thunder Canyon girls, head-ing for Rust Creek Falls looking for work—and maybe for love. They called it the Gal Rush, as I recall…"

The Gal Rush. Will remembered those awful ladies in Crawford's Sunday morning. He would not forget their snide remarks about the "Gal Rush women" descending on Rust Creek Falls to catch a cowboy.

But if the reference got to Jordyn, she didn't let it show.

She only shrugged and agreed with Desiree, "That's right. We were part of the Gal Rush—Jazzy, Cece and me."

Desiree swung her too-bright smile on Will. "And what about you, Will? What brings you to the area?"

He went ahead and told her. "I live here, too, now. I recently bought a ranch not far from Rust Creek Falls."

Desiree blinked. Twice. "You bought a ranch? Already?" Sudden tension vibrated in her voice, and her fake smile had fled. Jordyn glanced from Desiree to him and back to Desiree again.

Will fervently wished that Desiree would give it up and go away. He answered gently, "Circumstances change."

"Oh, well. I guess they do." She gave a quick shake of her dark curls, and her lips tipped up in that too-bright smile again. "I'm here for a week or two, helping my aunt Georgina pack her things." She flicked out a hand in the direction of a table by the window, where a sweet-looking gray-haired lady sat happily working her way through a big plate of pasta. "Aunt Georgie's been failing lately. She was having trouble looking out for herself, so we're moving her back to Thunder Canyon and into assisted living."

Jordyn's blue eyes were much too watchful. Will figured she'd probably heard from Cece that he and Desiree once had a thing. And right now Jordyn had to have gotten the picture that Desiree wasn't exactly at peace with the way it had all turned out. "It's, um, good you could come and help your aunt." Jordyn nervously smoothed a loose strand of hair back up into her ponytail.

That was when it happened: Desiree spotted Jordyn's ring. A tiny gasp escaped her. She shifted her narrowed gaze on Will again. He went ahead and lifted his left hand to grab his water glass for a leisurely sip, giving her plenty of time to confirm her suspicion that he wore a ring, too.

Desiree asked, "Why do I get the feeling that congratulations are in order?"

Will set down his glass. "Thanks, Desiree. Jordyn and I were married last Saturday."

"Oh, really?"

Jordyn sailed into the breach. "That's right. Will and I are newlyweds."

A silence. Desiree hovered on the brink—of what, he wasn't sure. But in the end, she only said, "I...hope you'll both be very happy."

"Thanks," Jordyn replied softly. "We are."

Desiree's red lips twisted. "Well, um, great to see you both. You take care now."

"You, too," Jordyn said.

Will nodded. "See you, Desiree."

And that was it. Desiree turned away at last. She marched across the room and rejoined her aunt.

The rest of the meal went by fast, with hardly another word shared between him and Jordyn. She seemed not to know what to say. And he didn't want to get into all that old business, anyway.

They finished. He paid the check, and they left for home.

Once they were on the road, Jordyn asked softly, "Are you all right, Will?"

"Fine."

She sent him a quick, unhappy glance. "You don't seem fine."

"I *said* I was fine. Can we leave it at that?" He said it harshly, taking the offensive when she didn't deserve it, a ploy to end this conversation before it really began.

At first she was quiet. He dared to hope he'd been a big enough jerk that she would *stay* quiet. But she'd never lacked guts. She tried again. "I remember you went out with her. Cece mentioned you were dating her more than once. My mom mentioned it, too. And I know it was serious. Desiree seemed really upset back there. *You* didn't seem very happy, either..." Her voice trailed off. He dared to zip her a sideways glance. She had her hands folded in her lap, and she stared down at them, mouth set, soft chin tensed.

"Leave it alone, Jordyn. It's not a big deal."

She kept staring at her hands. "You're doing a crap job of lying to me right now, Will."

"Leave it." He growled the words.

Her bright head shot up. She looked straight at him. "Well, alrighty, then."

The rest of the ride was as silent as the end of the meal had been.

At the ranch she made a beeline for the kitchen.

He followed her in there. She zipped over to the counter and got to work unpacking the grocery bags they'd left there.

"Leave that stuff," he said. "I'll deal with it tomorrow. Don't you have homework you need to be doing?"

She had a jar of peanut butter in one hand and a can of cocoa in the other. "I'll just—"

"I said leave it, Jordyn." Maybe it came out a little gruffer than it should have.

She glared at him. Then she stuck both items in a cupboard, shut the cupboard door and put up her hands like he held her at gunpoint. "Fine."

"What about your homework?"

She pressed her lips together. He was certain she would say something snippy. But in the end, she took the high road. "I need to get online to do it. It's no biggie. I'll just stay at Country Kids for a couple of hours tomorrow after work. Sara has Wi-Fi." She added, defiantly, "So don't expect me until after five—or better make it six, to give me plenty of time to get it all done."

He should leave it alone. If she wanted to do her homework at Sara Johnston's, what the hell did it matter to him? But somehow, his big mouth opened all by itself, and he issued what sounded way too much like a command. "Tomorrow you'll do your homework here."

"What in the world is going on with you, Will?"

"You heard me. You can do your homework here."

"That is not what you said, and we both know it. You gave me an order, Will. You don't have any right to go giving me orders. Where I do my homework is my business. And anyway, I just told you that I *can't* do it here because there is no internet connection."

"Tomorrow, first thing, the satellite guys are hooking us up. We'll have TV and internet before noon."

Spots of hectic color flamed on her soft cheeks. "Oh. Well, great. Terrific. I'll just rush right back here after work."

"Good."

She bit her lower lip. "And right now I think I'll go out and check on the animals." She started for the back door.

He knew he should let her go. But instead he reached out and caught her arm as she tried to brush past him. "Anything to get away from me, huh?"

She froze, blinked down at his fingers wrapped around her arm and then back up at him. Something arced between them, something bright and hot. And dangerous, too. "I didn't say that."

"You didn't *have* to say it." He liked the feel of her smooth skin against his palm, liked it too much. Reluctantly, he released her.

"Are you finished?" She held her ground, waiting for him to stop being an ass and say something real.

So he did. "I just don't want to talk about Desiree."

"Then don't." She headed for the door again.

He ached to call her back. But then she would expect him to actually talk to her.

And he was not up for that.

So he just stood there feeling like ten kinds of hopeless SOB as she went out the back door.

Chapter Eight

Jordyn had a nice long chat with the goats. They agreed that Will was a great big butthead. She spent some time with Mama Kitty and her babies, fussing over them.

When she went back inside, Will had left the kitchen. The door to the master suite was shut, a sliver of light shining beneath it. Terrific. He could be a jackass all by his lonesome, locked in his room. Fine with her.

Feeling equal parts defiant and helpful, she put away the rest of the groceries he'd bought and unboxed the microwave, the mixer, the slow cooker and the electric can opener. She folded all the bags and put them under the sink next to the trash can, then broke down the boxes.

After that she went upstairs and spent the rest of the evening alone.

In the morning they ate breakfast in silence. She put a pot roast and veggies in the slow cooker for dinner and then headed for work without saying two words to him.

That afternoon when she returned, she spotted cattle grazing on the hill above the stock pond. The beginnings of Will's herd must have arrived.

A circle of dusty pickups waited in front of the house. She recognized them as belonging to Will's brothers. But inside, the house was quiet. They must all be out working, getting the cattle settled in, mending fences and who knew what all.

Which was great. She had homework to do, anyway—that was, if in fact Will now had Wi-Fi, as he'd been so sure he would last night. The big-screen TV over the fireplace seemed a good sign. And the TV wasn't the only new addition. A leather sofa, coffee table and two comfy chairs made the living room a lot more inviting. In the utility room, she found a brand-new washer and dryer, hooked up and ready to go. There was also a new table and six chairs in the breakfast nook.

When it came to getting things done, Will did not fool around. She might almost admire him—if she wasn't so pissed off at him.

The billy goat must have heard her drive up. He was crying like a baby, as usual. Chuckling to herself, she went to work feeding the goats and the lone rooster. She'd stopped in at Crawford's for cat food, so she fed the mama cat and petted all the kittens.

Back inside, she went upstairs, where she discovered a sticky note on her bedroom door. *Wi-Fi operational*, Will had scrawled in his bold hand, along with the necessary password. She kicked off her shoes, got comfy on the bed and got started on her homework.

At a little before six, she heard the men come in downstairs. She might have stayed in her room for a couple more hours just to avoid playing dueling silent treatments with

Will, but she liked his brothers, and it would be rude not to go down and say hi.

She found the Clifton men in the kitchen, each with a beer, all in stocking feet with their faces and hands freshly scrubbed. Carol Clifton had raised them right. Those boys knew to wash up when they came in the house, and to leave their muddy boots at the door.

Craig, the oldest, had the lid off the slow cooker. "Jordyn Leigh, this smells great. Will's a lucky man."

The lucky man in question sipped his beer and said nothing.

Jordyn avoided Will's eyes and told his brother, "Thanks, Craig. Great to see you."

Rob, the youngest, grabbed her and spun her around. "Are you nuts, Jordyn Leigh, to go and marry *him*?"

"Robbie!" She kissed his scruffy cheek. "I think I might have lost my mind for a moment there—and how you been?"

"Can't complain. You're beautiful, as always."

Will muttered something under his breath. Jordyn didn't hear what, which was probably just as well.

She laughed. "Oh, Rob. I know you're just after my pot roast."

Rob confessed, "Well, it does smell mighty fine."

Jonathan, third born after Will, pulled her close next. "Will gives you any trouble, you let me know. I'll adjust his attitude for you."

She hugged him back. "I can always count on you, Jonathan."

Will cleared his throat. "So. Dinner ready?"

She turned to him, really tempted to say something caustic in response. But his brothers were watching—and besides, she had another way to get under his skin. She went to him, put her hands on his big, hard shoulders and smiled up at him sweetly. "Yep. Dinner's ready. Someone just needs to put it on the table."

He kept his hands at his sides and looked down at her, suspicion in his eyes. "Great. We'll do that."

"Thanks." She couldn't resist playing the moment for all it was worth. "So, honey, how was your day?"

His eyes turned turbulent, and his square jaw twitched—and then he moved, reaching. His warm hands slid around her waist and came to rest at the small of her back. Dear Lord, for someone so annoying, he was such a big ol' hunk of pure manliness. "It was a good day," he said gruffly. "Got a lot done."

"I noticed." She smiled wider, and he volunteered some actual information. "Several head of cattle arrived. I bought them at auction last week."

"I spotted a few of them on the ridge above the stock pond when I drove up."

His right hand moved at her back, a slow glide that could only be called a caress. She felt powerful, suddenly, her blood racing swift and hot through her veins, a warm, lovely shiver moving over her skin. She let her gaze stray to his mouth. His lips were so full and soft compared to the rest of him.

Now *he* was staring at *her* mouth. She held her breath. And then those big arms closed around her, and his dark head came down. He smelled so good—a hint of soap and warm, healthy skin.

And his kiss? Spectacular. It made heat bloom in her belly and her knees feel wobbly. No wonder Desiree Fenton was still bitter that she'd lost him.

When he lifted his head, she felt branded, as though his big body had imprinted itself all down the front of hers. They stared at each other, partly in anger—but anger wasn't all of it. Not by a long shot. Heat still lingered, burning between them.

It was only a kiss, she reminded herself. A nice little public display of affection, for the sake of their newlywed act.

Jonathan teased, "Okay, you two. Any more of that and you really need to get a room."

That broke the tension. Everybody laughed.

Jordyn pushed at Will's rock-hard chest. He let her go. She said, "All right, boys. Get the table set. I'll put the food on."

The Clifton brothers ate heartily. Once the meal was cleared off, they all sat around and visited for an hour or so. At seven-thirty, the boys headed back to Maverick Manor, promising to return the next morning. Tomorrow would be another busy day at the Flying C. The new foreman and his wife would arrive from Thunder Canyon. Also scheduled to show up tomorrow: a moving van of Will's furniture and the three horses he owned.

With the brothers gone, the house seemed way too quiet. It was just Jordyn and Will, with the bad feelings from last night like an invisible wall between them. Jordyn got to work on the dishes.

Will grabbed the towel and started drying.

More silence. He was the one who finally broke it. "I bought a dishwasher yesterday, when I bought the washer and dryer. You see the washer and dryer?"

She didn't really want to fight with him anymore. But she didn't feel kindly toward him, either. So she answered flatly, "I did. Looks good."

"The dishwasher will be installed tomorrow."

She rinsed a soapy dish. "Great."

"You, uh, get the password all right, for the Wi-Fi?"

"I did, thanks." She handed him the rinsed dish.

He dried it and set it on the stack he'd made beside the dish rack. "Your homework?"

"All done." She washed and rinsed the last dish. He dried it and put it on the stack. She got going on the glassware. He dried each one and put them away.

Eventually, he tried again. "The Realtor called back. About the goats and the cats and that rooster?"

"Yeah?"

"The former owners have no place for animals where they live now. The Realtor said they're 'in no position' to deal with any leftover livestock. Long story short, I own three goats, a mama cat with kittens, a bad-tempered, self-important rooster—and whatever other critter shows up at the back door."

Jordyn said nothing to that. What was there to say? She felt a flicker of satisfaction at the news. After all, she actually liked the critters in question. But in the end, she reminded herself, she shouldn't get too attached. She would have to walk away from them when she left for Missoula. They were his responsibility now, and he could do with them as he pleased.

Will set down the towel, carried the dried plates to the cabinet at the end of the counter and put them away. She slid him a glance when he just stood there, staring at the cabinet once he'd shut the door, his back to her.

Then, abruptly, he turned. "How long are you gonna be mad at me?" His beautiful mouth curved down at the corners, and his fine eyes were troubled.

Sudden warmth bloomed in the center of her chest, a definite tenderness toward him. She answered honestly, "Oh, probably until you talk to me." She grabbed the terry-cloth hand towel from its hook and wiped her hands.

He said, "We could go in the living room, sit on that couch I just bought..." He offered his hand.

She took it. His fingers closed around hers, and she felt better about everything.

In the living room, they sat at either end of the sofa. She kicked off her shoes and drew her legs up sideways, facing him.

He hitched one knee to the cushions, shifting his big body her way. "It's pretty simple," he said. "I was never getting married until I had my place. Desiree knew that when we started in together."

"You mean you told her that up front?"

"Yeah. And I told her how long that would be—at least fifteen years. At the time, I had no clue that we'd lose Aunt Willie in two years, so I was still working on my original schedule then. I was twenty-eight when Desiree and I started going out. And I generally tried to keep things honest and upfront with any woman I went with. I tried to have the talk with them early."

"Wow. There's an actual *talk*?"

"Yeah." He gave her a sideways look. "Does that sound bad or something?"

She blew out a breath. "I'm not sure..."

"Remember Brita Foxworth?"

Jordyn did remember. "You went with her in high school. Everyone thought you two would get married after graduation."

"Brita was planning our wedding by Senior Ball." He sounded weary. "I finally had to tell her that there wasn't going to be one. Not for years and years, anyway. Not until I got my place, which by my calculations then was going to be at the age of forty-five—maybe a couple years earlier, if I scrimped and saved and pinched every penny. Brita and I broke up right before graduation, the night that I finally got through to her that I wasn't marrying anyone for a long, long time. From then on, if I really liked a woman and wanted to see her more than a time or two, I made sure we had the talk good and early."

Jordyn shifted, stretching out an arm to rest it along the sofa back. "So you had the *talk* right at the first, with Desiree?"

"Yeah. And she said that was fine with her. She said she didn't want to get married, anyway."

"Hmm. Judging by the expression on her face yesterday when she put it together that you and I are married, she either lied or changed her mind."

Now he was the one shifting, facing forward, bracing both elbows on his spread knees. "We went out for almost a year, Desiree and me."

Jordyn winced. "I hadn't realized it lasted that long."

"Jordyn, I liked her. I had fun with her. I thought she was fine with the way things were. But then one night we went out to dinner, and we went back to her place. And suddenly, we were into this big scene. She was crying and telling me she loved me and she couldn't do it, couldn't wait anymore. She wanted to get married. She wanted us together in the way that really mattered. She wanted a ring, and she wanted it now."

"Did you...I mean, were you in love with her?" She asked the question and kind of wished she hadn't. If he said yes, the next question would have to be, *Are you still in love with her?* And Jordyn didn't know if she could bring herself to ask that one.

Okay, their marriage might be just for show, but some part of her kept growing more...invested every day. To learn that he still carried a torch for Desiree Fenton, well, that would make her feel awful on any number of levels.

And he was taking way too long to answer. "Will?" she prompted impatiently.

He finally put it out there. "I told you. I *liked* her. But I wasn't in love with her, and I didn't want to get married."

Relief. She felt relief. She decided not to think about that and to focus instead on what a thickheaded fool he'd been. "Men can be so clueless." Jordyn hadn't realized she'd said that out loud.

Not until he said, "Clueless? She never said anything for all those months and months. She acted like she was happy. And then, all of a sudden…she wasn't."

"I'm sure there were signs. You just refused to see them."

He threw up both hands. "Maybe. I don't know. I do know that I felt like a first-class jerk when it ended, and I felt like one again yesterday, at the sight of her. And right now, too, as a matter of fact. I really didn't mean to hurt her…"

She mimicked, *"I really didn't mean to hurt her."*

"Well, I didn't."

"And I need to embroider that on a sampler and hang it in your kitchen."

"All right, Jordyn. Why don't you just tell me, then. What the hell *should* I have done?"

That did give her pause. She confessed, "I don't know. Sometimes, in love, people just get hurt—and I think someone told me that after it ended with you, she went out with Roger Boudreaux and that he broke it off, too. So I'm guessing she's not real happy with your gender at this point in her life."

He braced his elbows on his knees again and hung his head. "I need a beer. You want one?"

"No, thanks."

He got up, disappeared into the kitchen and returned with a cold one. Dropping down beside her again, he took a long pull off the can. "So, you and me? We're okay now?"

She held his gaze for a moment and finally nodded. "Yeah. We're okay."

He let out a hard breath and slumped against the cushions. "That's a relief."

She considered their hasty marriage, told herself not to go there—and then went right ahead and brought it up, anyway. "Lucky you got this ranch before Saturday night, huh?"

He slid her a frown. "Why do you say that?"

"Think about it. What if you woke up married to me and you didn't have your place yet? A lifetime of big plans right down the drain."

"Jordyn…" He gave her a warning look.

Which she blithely ignored. "So after we're divorced, you'll be lookin', huh? Ready to find yourself a nice little wife—and fifteen years ahead of schedule, too. Ain't life grand?"

"Jordyn Leigh." That time he said it in his boss-man voice.

She made a show of batting her eyelashes and drawled, "What, Will?"

"I may be clueless, but even I know that finding the right person to spend my life with doesn't happen on a schedule. I know it's not like buying a couch or a big-screen TV."

She snickered in a way that she knew was nothing short of evil. "Will. You hopeless romantic, you."

"Don't mock me. I'm serious. Yeah, in a couple of years, after I've got this ranch up and running, I'll be looking. But I want it all. I'm not going to settle. I want what my folks have. What *your* parents have. Love with the one and only. I'm not taking less than that." His words made her heart hurt, which served her right for goading him in the first place. And he was watching her. "Okay. Now you look sad. What'd I do this time?"

She met his incomparable eyes and refused to look away. "Nothing."

"Come on." So sweet. So gentle. The man could coax the moon from the sky if he put his mind to it. "Tell me."

She gave in and admitted, "It was beautiful, what you just said, that's all."

His dark brows lifted, and he asked hopefully, "And beautiful is good?"

Now she felt shy and too young and way too tender. "Yeah. Beautiful is good."

A lock of inky hair fell across his forehead. Her fingers ached to brush it back.

But she didn't. That would be kind of intimate. And they didn't really do intimate—except when they had an audience.

He grabbed the remote off the coffee table. "You want to watch some TV?"

"Sure. Why not?"

The big screen over the fireplace burst into life. ESPN, of course, with a baseball game in progress. She liked baseball as much as the next girl, which was to say maybe not as much as some. But enough to sit on Will's new couch with him and cheer if somebody hit a home run.

He settled into the cushions and stretched his arm across the back of the sofa. His fingers brushed her shoulder. A little thrill shivered down her arm.

Get a grip, Jordyn Leigh.

"Come on," he said. "Make yourself comfortable."

She swayed toward him—because she wanted to, wanted to lean against him, have his arm around her, pretend...

Okay, never mind what she might want to pretend.

He aided and abetted her in her foolish desire, hooking that big, hard arm around her, drawing her against his side. She let herself lean into him.

And it felt really, really good.

Too good, she knew that. And too intimate, considering it was just the two of them on that sofa, no one else in the room to put on a show for.

"Better, huh?" he asked, giving her an extra squeeze.

"Yeah," she said, and snuggled closer still.

She woke up in the middle of the night, upstairs in her own bed, still wearing her jeans and T-shirt, with the blankets tucked in around her.

Will. What a guy.

She pushed back the blankets, took off her jeans, wiggled out of her bra, but left the T-shirt on. Then she settled back under the covers and drifted to sleep again, smiling to herself.

The next day was Friday.

When Jordyn got home from work, Will's brothers had already left for Maverick Manor. Will took her over to the foreman's cottage and introduced her to his new foreman, Myron Stevalik, and his wife, Pia. Jordyn liked them both and told Pia if she needed help with anything, just to let her know.

Pia thanked her for the offer and said that, so far, she was managing just fine. The three-bedroom cottage was a little dusty but clean, Pia added with some relief, and all the kitchen appliances worked. Jordyn and Will stayed only a few minutes, clearing out quickly so the couple could get back to putting their new home together.

The movers had come with the contents of the little house Will used to rent in Thunder Canyon. The front porch and the entry hall were crammed with furniture and stacks of boxes containing clothes and household goods.

Jordyn and Will worked together, sorting furniture and arranging it in the various rooms. They set up the king-size bed and matching dresser in the master suite and moved the bed he'd been using to the extra room upstairs.

Jordyn's room got a dresser, a couple of chairs and even a nightstand. She also got more towels for the upstairs bath and extra sheets. She helped carry the boxes of his personal stuff into the master suite, where he could deal with them whenever he found the time. And there were several boxes of kitchen stuff, too, as well as a nice big oak table and chairs for the dining room.

At a little after six, Jordyn took two servings of slow cooker chicken and dumplings across the yard to the Stevaliks. Pia called her a lifesaver and asked if Jordyn and Will might go with them to services at Rust Creek Falls Community Church on Sunday.

"It would be nice," said Pia, "to get to know our neighbors, to make some friends. And it would be so great if you and Will would introduce us to a few people in the congregation."

Jordyn reminded her, "Will's new to town, too."

"So you think he wouldn't want to go?"

"How about if I just ask him?" Jordyn did feel a little pang of discomfort at the prospect. Maybe God wouldn't approve of newlyweds with a Divorce Plan. But then again, God was all about love and forgiveness, and His doors were open to everyone. Jordyn went to church most Sundays, and she wasn't about to stop going just because her marriage wasn't everything most people thought it was.

Back at the main house, Will had the table set. They sat down, and she asked him if he would go to church with her and the Stevaliks that Sunday. He said he would, simple as that.

They ate and then put their dishes in the new dishwasher. Will went out to check on his horses, which had arrived that morning. Jordyn went back across the yard to tell Pia they were on for church on Sunday. She returned to the house and got back to work on the boxes of kitchen stuff.

When Will came inside at nine-thirty, she was putting various gadgets in drawers.

She held up a rotary egg beater, circa 1955, and spun the handle so the beaters whirled. "I think this may be an actual antique."

He came straight to the counter, whipped the half-empty box she'd been unloading out from under her nose, carried it over and plopped it on top of the dwindling stack of boxes in the corner.

"Will! I'm not finished with that."

"You are for tonight."

"But I just want to—"

"Uh-uh. You've done more than enough for one day."

They had made serious progress. The place was actually beginning to look kind of cozy. Yeah, it needed paint inside and out, and the kitchen could use a general upgrade. But still. It was comfortable now. And Jordyn felt some satisfaction that she'd pitched in to help make it so.

Will asked, "How about streaming a movie?"

A movie. That would be nice. Especially if he put his arm around her and let her use him as a pillow. She would cuddle up nice and close. And if she dropped off to sleep, he would carry her upstairs and put her to bed just like last night…

"Jordyn Leigh?" He was still waiting on her answer.

"Oh! Sorry." She realized she'd been standing there in front of the still-open gadget drawer, staring off into space.

She dropped the egg beater in the drawer and shoved it shut with more force than necessary. "You know, I'm kind of tired. I think I'll just go on upstairs."

"You sure?" Did he sound disappointed that she wouldn't stay and hang around with him? Or was that only wishful thinking on her part?

Didn't matter. Upstairs. She was going upstairs. "Uh, yeah. I could use a good night's sleep." She beamed him a huge smile—a smile that felt forced as it spread across her face.

And he knew it was forced. Twin lines formed between his dark brows. "Are you okay?"

"Fine, fine. A little tired is all."

He was still frowning, but at least he let it go.

She said good-night and went up the stairs and did not allow herself to weaken and go back down.

In the morning he was already outside tending the animals when she got up. She went to work on breakfast and when he came in, they ate.

He was halfway through his eggs and ham, when he suddenly looked up, snared her gaze across the table and asked, "So what's your plan for today?"

She sipped her coffee. "Finish unpacking the kitchen stuff, maybe get ahead on my homework…"

"How about a picnic?" He gave her that killer smile. "Just you and me. We'll go on horseback. The Flying C is the prettiest ranch in the Rust Creek Valley, and I want a chance to show you around."

It sounded like fun. And what kind of dangerous intimacy were they going to get up to on horses in the middle of the day?

She decided not to think too hard about that. "Yeah. Yeah, I'd like that."

"Wear something you can swim in. We'll be mostly

following the creek, and it's going to be hot today. I know of a great little swimming hole with its own waterfall. A swim should cool us off."

Cool them off. Yeah. She could use a little cooling off when it came to him.

"Er, Jordyn?"

She realized she was staring blankly at nothing again. "Hmm?"

"Bring a swimsuit?"

"Of course. Absolutely. I will."

At half past eleven she was mounted on Darlin', Will's dappled gray mare, with a plain lunch of sandwiches and fruit packed up in the saddlebags, wearing her swimsuit under her clothes. Will led the way on Shady, his favorite black gelding.

They circled the stock pond as several Black Angus heifers watched them from the ridge above. A curious steer tagged after them for a mile or so as they left the pond to follow the meandering ribbon of Badger Creek. At first, they rode in rolling grassland, staying beyond the stands of trees that lined the water's edge. The sun was warm on her back—a little too warm. Even after she tucked her hair up under her hat to let the wind cool her neck, she had a dew of moisture on her upper lip, and her shirt clung beneath her arms.

After a while they began to climb, following the general path of the creek up a steepening grade. Will led the way, taking them closer to creekside under the willows and cottonwoods. It was still hot, but at least the trees provided a little shade.

Ahead, she could hear a low, continuous roar. "I think I hear that waterfall of yours," she called.

He waved a hand, signaling her forward, and she moved

up to ride beside him. As they wound through the trees, he said, "It's just up ahead..."

"I could use a swim."

His mouth curled up beneath the brim of his hat. "Me, too."

The sound of the water grew louder. They rounded the next bend, and he guided them off the trail, through the trees to the water's edge.

"Here we are." He sounded pleased.

And he should be. The waterfall splashed down the giant black rocks on the other side into a clear green pool. "It's beautiful."

He looked so pleased with himself. "I kinda thought you might like it."

They hobbled the horses and drank from their canteens. Then they spread a saddle blanket on the bank and stripped down—she to her Hawaiian-print two-piece, Will to his Wranglers.

He hit the water at a run.

She was right behind him, diving in, ducking her head under, letting out a shout when she surfaced. "It's cold!"

He laughed. "Come on..." He struck out for the black rocks on the other bank.

She swam after him, following him to a spot where they could climb out of the water and up the slippery rocks. He started upward, careful of his footing. She came after him, putting her feet and hands where he put his. Twice she squealed when her foot slipped.

He stopped and grinned back at her both times. "You need help?"

"Are you kidding? I know what I'm doing."

He only shook his head and kept climbing. At the top, he boosted himself to the ledge of black rock and held his hand down to her. She almost huffed at him that she could do it herself—because old habits die hard, and she'd spent what seemed like all of her childhood telling Will Clifton that he wasn't the boss of her, and she didn't need his help.

But then she couldn't help chuckling at her own child-ishness. She reached up, and he curled his strong fingers around hers. He gave a tug, rising to his feet, and up she went, landing on the ledge beside him, laughing some more as she stumbled a little.

He wrapped her in his big arms to steady her. "Care-ful—and what's so funny?"

She gazed up into those eyes—pale blue rimmed in a blue so deep—and suddenly, it wasn't funny. Nothing was funny. His wet, slicked-back hair gleamed blue-black, and beads of water glistened on the fine, sculpted angles of his handsome face, on the powerful musculature of his broad shoulders and deep chest. She wanted to stand there for at least a century or two, caught in that shaft of warm sunlight that streamed through a gap in the trees, with his hard, wet arms around her.

"Jordyn?"

"Hmm?"

"You're doing it again."

"Um, doing what?"

"Staring. Not hearing me when I speak to you. A mil-lion miles away…"

"No," she heard herself say softly. "Really. I'm right here." She stared at his mouth, acutely aware that if she kissed him now, there was absolutely no way she could excuse the move as a PDA. No one was watching—well, maybe the horses, but they sure didn't care. If she kissed him, it would be a real kiss. It would be because she *wanted* to kiss him—and she did.

She wanted that, a lot.

Vague memories of last Saturday night seemed to swirl

in the air between them. Was it only a week ago, when they danced in the park under the moon, when they stood together in front of the judge?

Was it only last Sunday that she woke up wearing a wedding ring?

"Jordyn?" His mouth, somehow, seemed to get even softer, fuller than before, creating a sharper contrast to the rest of him, to the sexy dark stubble on his cheeks and jaw, to all those lean, honed muscles, those strong arms wrapped around her nice and tight.

And why did he always have to smell so good? That really wasn't fair.

Again, he asked, "Jordyn?"

And that time, she remembered to answer. "Will." She said it very softly, like a secret. Or a prayer. And she reached up, sliding her open hand over his beautiful, hard, wet chest, curling her fingers around the back of his strong neck, brushing the blunt, wet ends of his black hair. "Will…"

He answered her in a rough whisper, "Jordyn."

And his mouth came down to meet hers.

Chapter Nine

William covered her sweet, tempting lips with his.

Perfect, those lips of hers. Just as they'd been the other night, when she'd kissed him in front of his brothers. And at Crawford's last week, when he'd kissed her for the benefit of those two gossiping ladies.

And last Saturday night, when he'd kissed her just because he wanted to.

Little Jordyn Leigh Cates. Best kisser ever.

He should be over his surprise at how good her lips tasted. But he wasn't. He had a feeling he might never get over how terrific kissing her felt. Every time it happened, it felt like the first time.

He hoped it happened a lot in these few weeks they had together, whether he ought to be hoping that or not.

Her slim body felt just right in his arms. And best of all, she wasn't pulling away—even though they had no audience to play newlyweds for. She was kissing him back.

His wet jeans got tighter as those fine lips parted and she let him in for a deeper taste. So damn sweet.

And *his*.

His wife.

Yeah, okay. Only temporarily.

But maybe not. Maybe more than kissing had happened Saturday night. And if it had, just maybe, she was going to have his baby.

And if there *was* a baby coming, well, they'd already agreed that they would stay together, work it out, the two of them, as a married couple.

Okay, maybe a baby wasn't all that likely, no matter what they'd done Saturday night.

But so what?

Right now life was good. He was still kissing her. And she was definitely into it.

He let his hands roam the silky, wet skin of her back. Her firm little breasts felt so good pressing into his chest— even with her swimsuit top in the way. The scent of her filled his head. Ripe peaches, spring rain. She made him dizzy in the best possible way.

He tottered on the ledge. "Whoa," he growled against her parted lips. "Come on down…"

She sighed, her breath warm and sweet across his cheek. "You mean, before we fall down?"

"Yes, I do." He covered her mouth again and drank her in, nipping at her lower lip then soothing it with a slow glide of his tongue. As he kissed her, he bent his legs and carried her down with him, turning her and settling her across his thighs on the rocky ledge—and trying not to groan as his soggy jeans pinched his groin.

She leaned back on his cradling arm and touched his cheek with her fingers, stroking so lightly. "We shouldn't be doing this…"

He caught her index finger between his lips, teased it with his tongue and reluctantly let it go. "Shh. It's okay. We're just…"

"What?" Big trusting eyes held his. "We're just what?"

"Fooling around a little." He brushed his hand down her arm, loving the silky feel of her skin beneath his palm. "No harm done…"

She made a sweet humming sound low in her throat and touched his face again, fingertips skimming the scruff on his cheeks. "You're sure about that?"

"Of course I'm sure." He sounded so confident. What a joke. He should tell her the truth, admit that he wasn't sure about anything.

Not since last Saturday night.

His jeans were tight and getting tighter. But so what?

He was only going to kiss her and hold her a little. And there really was no harm in that. It was nothing they hadn't done before.

"Will…"

By way of an answer, he captured her upturned mouth for another kiss, a long one. She stiffened at first—but then she gave in and kissed him back.

When he finally lifted his lips from hers, she cuddled against him and tucked her head under his chin. Shyly, she told him, "You're a really good kisser, Will."

"I was just thinking the same thing about you."

She giggled, an adorable, delighted little sound. "No. Seriously."

"Yeah. Seriously." He gathered the dripping coils of her long hair and wrapped them around his hand. "I think we've got chemistry, Jordyn Leigh."

She looked up at him, all big eyes and soft just-kissed lips. "I think so, too. And I mean, who would ever have guessed? You and me, like this, together? You were always such a pain in the butt."

He kissed her, a quick one. "You don't mean that."

"Oh, yes, I do. And all the girls would talk about you, about how hot you are. And I was always like, 'Oh, I know, he's really handsome, sure, and he can be so charming when he wants to be and what girl in her right mind doesn't love a cowboy? But you don't know him like I do...'"

He answered carefully, "I think I'm going to focus on the part about how you think I'm handsome and charming."

"Yeah, right. You do that." She dipped her head beneath his chin again.

With slow care, he uncoiled her hair from around his palm. "Hey."

"Hmm?"

"Look at me."

"No."

"Come on..."

"Uh-uh."

"Uh-huh."

And she gave in and glanced up.

He was ready for her. He swooped in and captured her lips again. This time she gasped a little against his mouth. He drank in that startled sound and went on kissing her, taking his time.

A long time...

By the end of that kiss, he was aching to do a lot more than kiss her.

She leaned back in his arms and stared up at him, lips cherry red, cheeks slightly flushed. "We probably should cut this out, huh?"

Cutting it out was the last thing he wanted to do. But he knew she was right. "Yes, I think we should." And he made himself follow through, gently scooping her up in his arms and setting her on the ledge beside him. "There."

She leaned her head on his shoulder. For a while they were silent together. Finally, she said, "It's nice here—the falls, the swimming hole, this spot in the sun."

"I thought you'd like it." He captured her hand and wove his fingers with hers. "Come on." He gathered his legs beneath him and stood. She rose with him. "Let's ride down the falls."

Carefully, they made their way across the slippery rocks, over to where the water poured free of the wide ledge, falling in a white, foaming spray into the pool below.

"You first," he offered.

She didn't even hesitate, just let go of his hand and picked her way through the rushing water to the middle of the stream. Once she got there, she sat down—and slid off the edge.

Holding her arms high, she squealed as she fell, landing butt first in the pool below, sinking under the surface, pink-painted toes last—and then shooting up out of the churning water with a loud, "Whoa! What a ride!"

He waited until she cleared the waterfall, all that gold hair streaming behind her. Then he made his way across the swift current to follow her down. They climbed the rocks twice more and rode the waterfall into the pool below.

When they got out on the trail side, their blanket was waiting under a tree. She took a comb from her saddlebag and corralled her wet hair into one thick braid down her back. They ate their sandwiches and munched on apples, then stretched out on the blanket side by side to let her suit and his jeans dry a little more before putting on the rest of their clothes for the ride back to the house.

It was peaceful in the dappled shade of the tree, with the soft roar of the falls across the creek. And it had been a long, busy week. He dozed for a while and woke to the sound of the wind stirring the branches above them. He rolled his head and looked at Jordyn. She lay on her back and seemed to be sleeping. He admired the soft curve of her mouth, became fascinated by the way her gold-tipped eyelashes fanned across her smooth cheeks.

And then, as if she could feel the weight of his gaze on her, she turned her head and opened her eyes halfway. "Will." She smiled at him.

He couldn't resist. He levered up on an elbow and bent over her. "Tell me not to kiss you again."

She didn't tell him any such thing. On the contrary, she lifted one hand and cupped the back of his head, her soft, cool fingers threading up into his hair. "Will…"

The invitation in her half-shut eyes tempted him powerfully—enough that he decided there really was no reason he needed to resist. He lowered his mouth and he kissed her, a long kiss, slow and deep, a kiss that tasted like apples and sunshine. A kiss that only led to another kiss.

And another after that.

With a happy little hum of sound, she turned her pretty body toward him. They lay on their sides, facing each other, her slim, cool hand moving over him, caressing his shoulder, his chest, the back of his neck. Her bare knees brushed his legs, setting off sparks even through his damp jeans. She kissed him so eagerly and murmured encouragements, "Will…yes…oh, yes…"

He touched her, too, running his hand into the dip of her waist, and up over the sleek outward curve of her hip. And he didn't stop there. On he went, his fingers gliding down the outside of her thigh—and back up again.

Her skin was so smooth, warm from the sun, dusted with baby-fine, barely there golden hair. He couldn't get enough of the feel of her under his hand. He ran his fingers down her spine, reaching the back strap of her suit top and resenting it mightily. But he was past that quickly, following her smooth skin on down—only to encounter the barrier of her suit bottom.

He really wanted her bare.

Bare. Yeah. He wanted *all* of her bare.

He went on kissing her, losing himself in the taste and the sweet, clean scent of her. And by then, it seemed the most natural thing in the world to let his hand glide back up again to the clasp at the strap of her suit top. It was the work of a few seconds to get it unhooked. Just a flick of his thumb and index finger...

Jordyn gasped, bringing up her hand between them to keep the top from falling off.

That woke him up. They pulled back at the same time and stared at each other, both of them breathing hard.

Her eyes had a dazed look, and her mouth was plump from his kisses. "I, um, really don't know if we should..." The words died in her throat.

The ability to speak seemed to have temporarily deserted him. He gaped at her, shocked at himself. Great way to look after little Jordyn Leigh. Take her for a ride and get her out of her swimsuit. What was the matter with him? He shouldn't be let out in public without supervision.

Damning himself for a low-down dirty dog, he sat up. "Get up and turn around." He said it way too gruffly.

She pushed herself up to a sitting position but didn't turn. Instead, she continued to stare at him, her eyes wide—with hurt. "Will. Why are you mad at me? What'd I do?"

"You didn't do anything." He made a real effort to speak more gently. "And I'm not mad at you, I'm mad at myself. I shouldn't have been kissing you—and I damn sure shouldn't be taking off your suit."

"It's okay." One of her shoulder straps fell down her arm. She pressed the top of the suit harder against her breasts to keep them covered. Damn, she looked good, all flushed and flustered, that mouth of hers so plump and sweet. In a sad little whisper, she insisted, "You didn't do anything wrong."

"The hell I didn't." He barked the words at her. She made a startled, wounded sound. He wanted to grab her and hold her and promise her it would be okay. But he knew where that would lead—to more kisses, more caresses, more opportunities to get her out of her swimsuit.

Uh-uh. She might be one fine kisser, but she was also a virgin. Or she had been until a week ago. He was supposed to be looking out for her and making up for whatever might have happened between them last Saturday night, not trying to get her out of her clothes.

"Turn around," he commanded, more harshly than he should have. "I'll hook you back up."

Still holding the top of the suit in place, she gathered her pretty legs to the side and turned her body, showing him her back, which was slim and soft and tempting, just like the rest of her. "I…I was just thinking that we ought to stop, is all. That things were maybe going a little further than they should—that is, I mean," she stammered adorably, "that you and me, together this way, well, it wasn't really in the plan."

"Damn right it wasn't." He got hold of both dangling straps as she reached back to catch her damp braid and guide it over her shoulder, out of his way. He hooked the straps together again. "There."

She fiddled with the shoulder straps and tugged on the front a little, adjusting it to cover her. "Thank you." Slowly, she turned around and faced him. "See? No harm done." A pretty blush flowed upward over her velvety cheeks.

He looked at her, so sweet and sexy, with her mouth still swollen from his kisses, beard burn reddening her tender skin—and all he wanted was to start kissing her again. "We should get going."

"If you're upset," she said in that prim little voice she used when she lectured him, "I think we should talk it over. You shouldn't be so hard on yourself. Nothing has happened here that I wasn't okay with."

"I'm not upset," he lied. Because there was no damn way he wanted to talk about it. What good would talking do? Except to get him angrier at himself than he already was. "Come on. Let's go."

For a minute she just sat there, watching him with a hurt and chiding expression. He knew she wouldn't let it go. She would start lecturing him about how they needed to hash it out, that communication mattered and all that crap.

But then, without a word, she grabbed her jeans from the edge of the blanket and started getting dressed. Relieved that she'd given it up, he pulled on his shirt and boots, and set his hat on his head. They packed up what was left of the lunch. He rolled the blanket and hooked it behind his saddle. They mounted up and started back.

He took the lead. The ride to the house was uneventful. And neither of them said a word the whole way.

At the house, Will told her he'd take care of the horses. Jordyn left him and went inside.

She had plenty to do. She made mac and cheese with ham for dinner and popped it in the oven. While it baked, she put away what was left of the kitchen stuff. Will never came in. Apparently, he had something important to do outside.

After what had happened at the swimming hole, she felt all edgy and strange. It had been so good, kissing Will, sitting on his lap up by the falls—lying with him on the blanket and kissing him some more. She couldn't help kind of wishing that she hadn't stopped him, that she'd just gone on kissing him, while he took away her top and then the suit bottom and then, well, wherever things had gone next. She had a feeling it would have been lovely.

But then, really, was that what she wanted? After all these years of telling herself that someday she would find someone special, someone to give both her heart and her body to?

No. Really. Making love with Will, no matter how good it felt, wouldn't be right.

Why not? asked a defiant, yearning voice in the back of her mind.

Good question. Because the really odd thing was that somewhere deep down inside herself, she had started thinking that making love with Will would be very, very right.

And that got her all confused all over again—maybe even more confused than she'd been when she woke up married to him last Sunday morning. She didn't want to feel confused, thank you very much.

So she decided *not* to think about it. She would just go about the rest of her day and forget what had happened at the swimming hole.

After she finished with the kitchen stuff, she took the mac and cheese out of the oven and left it on the stove with the lid on to cool a little. She got the salad ready and stuck it in the fridge. Then she went upstairs and did homework until she was three assignments ahead of where she needed to be on Monday.

When she came back down at six, she found the lid off the mac and cheese and a big hole in the middle of it. Half the salad was gone.

Will had left her a note on the counter. *Going into town for a beer with Craig and Rob. Back late. Don't wait up.*

Really? And to think she'd called him charming back at the swimming hole. Not to mention, let him kiss her until her clothes started falling off. She had to be out of her mind to even imagine that she might want to make love for the first time in her whole life with him—or possibly the second time, depending on what had happened Saturday night.

The jerk. He'd be lucky if she ever spoke to him again.

Will met his brothers at the Ace in the Hole on Sawmill Street. They drank beer and played pool, and he tried to forget the feel of Jordyn's soft lips on his, the scent of her skin, the joy on her pretty face as she shot down the falls.

Craig asked him why he hadn't brought Jordyn to town with him. He muttered something vague in reply. Rob pulled him aside and told him how happy he was for him.

"You got it all now, man," Rob said. "That sweet ranch and Jordyn Leigh, too."

"Thanks," Will said in a tone meant to end the conversation.

Rob didn't take the hint. "I always kind of had a secret thing for Jordyn Leigh. But you know how she is—not easy for a guy to get close to. The way she can look at a guy, like she has a pretty good idea of what's going on inside his head. That used to freak me out a little. And I always felt like she never took me seriously the times I tried to work up the nerve to ask her out."

Will suggested in a low growl, "Tell me you didn't just say you had a secret thing for my wife."

Rob arched an eyebrow and backed away. "Whoa, man. Jealous much?"

"I'm considering punching you in the face."

Rob grunted. "The hell you are. If you were gonna hit me, you'd have done it by now."

"Don't ever tell me that again."

"I was only sayin'—"

"I don't care. Don't say it again."

"Sheesh. Who put the burr under your blanket?"

Will didn't answer. Over at the pool table, Craig had missed his shot. Will picked up his pool cue, gave his baby brother one last dirty look and turned for the table.

By ten, he couldn't take it anymore. He felt like a complete SOB—probably because he was acting like one. He shouldn't have just eaten that nice dinner Jordyn cooked, left her that curt note and disappeared while she was still upstairs. What kind of guy did stuff like that?

An SOB, that's who.

"I'm heading home," he told his brothers.

Rob grinned. "Give Jordyn Leigh a big kiss for me."

Will felt his lip curl—and not in a smile. "You are just beggin' for it, aren't you?"

Rob made kissy noises.

Will turned and left before he lost it and beat the crap out of his own flesh and blood.

At the ranch the lights were still on downstairs. Will stopped the quad cab in the dark, a ways back from the house. He turned off the engine and sat there for a while, feeling like a first-class loser, knowing he had to go in and make amends, afraid he'd only mess things up worse when he tried to make them better.

But he couldn't sit out here in the dark forever. Finally, he made himself get out and go in the house.

The TV was on in the living room. He could see the big screen flickering through the front window. It went off when he let himself in the front door. He pushed the door shut behind him as Jordyn got up from the sofa and came to stand in the arch between the front hall and the living room.

"Will." She wore jeans and a little pink T-shirt, her wheat-gold hair loose on her shoulders. Her face was set, her eyes full of mutiny. She said, much too pleasantly, "You're home earlier than I expected."

He opened his mouth—and curt words came out. "I told you not to wait up."

She tipped her head to the side. Her shining hair tumbled down her arm. And then she folded both arms over those breasts he wanted so badly to see naked. "I was going to do exactly what you said in your note. Just go upstairs and not come down tonight," she said, her tone so calm and reasonable, it made him want to break something. "In fact, I was considering not speaking to you again for an extended period of time. But then I thought that would just be childish, that what I really needed to do was to wait for you to come home so we could work this out tonight."

He opened his mouth again—and shut it before he could lie and insist that there was nothing to work out.

She left the archway and came toward him, her bare feet with their pink-painted toes whispering across the plank floor. "You have something to say?"

Yeah, I want to kiss you some more. I want to do all kinds of things to you, and I want to do them now. "I..." That was as far as he got. He was an idiot, no doubt about it.

Her face softened. She was such a fine woman. Better than he would ever deserve, that was for sure. "I'm listening." She said it gently, though he'd done nothing at all to warrant her kindness. "Go ahead."

His mind went blank. Stalling for time, he took off his hat, turned and hung it on the hook by the door.

When he faced her again, she hadn't moved. She was

still just standing there, still so pretty it almost hurt to look at her—and still waiting for him to say what he had to say.

There was nothing for him to do but buck up and take a crack at an apology. "I was disgusted with myself for my behavior at the swimming hole. Instead of owning up to that, I took it out on you. That made me feel even madder at myself. I sent you inside and took care of the horses by myself so that I could have a little time to figure out how to tell you I was sorry. Then, the longer I stayed outside, the harder it got to think about facing you—so when I came in and you were still upstairs, I took the world's fastest shower, put a big dent in that excellent pot of macaroni and cheese you made for our dinner, zipped off that mean note and got the hell out."

When he stopped speaking, the front hall seemed to echo with silence. But at least she was still standing there. At least she hadn't turned on her heel and headed up the stairs.

She asked, "Is that all?"

He shrugged. "Rob has a crush on you. And I'm sorry, Jordyn Leigh. I'm really sorry for the way I've behaved."

She looked at him for what seemed like half a century. Finally, she said quietly, "I accept your apology."

His heart seemed to bounce toward his throat. "Er, you do?"

"Yes, I do." She offered her hand.

He took it, fast, before she could come to her senses and change her mind about forgiving him. He wrapped his fingers around her slim ones—and suddenly everything was right with the world. "Whew."

She chuckled. "You think I let you off too easy?"

"Yeah. Probably." He reached up, ran his other hand down her shining, silky hair. She let him do it, too, gazing up at him with trust in those beautiful china-blue eyes.

"Thank you," he said, his voice ragged and low.

"You're welcome. You want a beer or some coffee?"

"Coffee sounds good."

"Come on, then." She led him to the kitchen.

He put the water in the coffeemaker. She popped in the filter and spooned in the grounds. They stood together at the counter as it brewed, neither of them saying anything, which was fine. Words seemed unnecessary right then. It was just the two of them in the kitchen, waiting for the coffee to brew, and that was enough.

They filled their mugs and sat in the breakfast nook.

"I'll be awake half the night," she said ruefully, "drinking caffeine at this hour." She took a big sip, anyway. And then she set the mug down and wrapped her hands around it the way she had last Sunday morning in Kalispell, when he took her to that little restaurant for breakfast and they made their Divorce Plan. "And what do you mean, Rob has a crush on me?"

Why had he mentioned that? He had no idea. "I don't know what you're talking about."

She drank more coffee. "There's no point in saying you're sorry if you're only going to turn right around and tell me a lie."

He gave in and busted to the truth. "I don't know. He was giving me a hard time tonight, saying how I had it all, the ranch I'd always dreamed of—and you. Then he said he'd always had a thing for you, but you never took him seriously."

"Rob had a thing for me?" She waved a hand in front of her face. "Oh, come on. You know Rob. He was just giving you a hard time."

"So I probably shouldn't have threatened to knock his teeth out, huh?"

"Will." She sat up straighter in her chair. "You didn't…?"

"Actually beat the crap out of him? No, I only threatened to—and you're right. He was probably just joking around." Will didn't know if he believed that or not. But what did it matter? If Rob actually had considered asking her out, well, it was too late now. No Clifton alive would move in on another man's woman—especially not his own brother's wife.

But what happens when she's not your wife anymore?

Better not to even go there.

And so what if Rob had a crush on Jordyn Leigh? Who wouldn't have a crush on Jordyn Leigh? She was smart and pretty, and she had a good heart.

And he might as well face it. Rob wasn't the only one who had a thing for Jordyn Leigh. What had happened at the creek that day had forced him to admit that *he* wanted her. Bad. Odds were he was never going to have her. And that messed with his mind.

"Will?"

"Yeah?"

"Is something still bothering you?"

Now, what was he supposed to say to that? The truth would just get him deeper into territory he didn't want to explore. And a lie was plain wrong.

So he hedged. "I'm okay, really. I still feel bad about… everything that happened, that's all."

It worked. She told him softly, "Let it go. We're fine now."

Jordyn thoroughly enjoyed the rest of that evening. They took second cups of coffee into the living room and streamed a movie. Will let her choose a romantic comedy. He watched the whole thing and even seemed to enjoy it. She kind of wanted his arm around her, but he didn't offer. And after what had happened at the swimming hole, well, maybe cuddling up close to him was only asking for trouble. After the movie, she went upstairs to bed. And even with two cups of coffee buzzing through her system, she went to sleep as soon as her head hit the pillow.

Cece called her the next morning while she and Will were having breakfast and invited them over to her place for dinner that night. Will nodded when Jordyn passed on the invitation, so she told Cece they would be there.

They caravanned into town with the Stevaliks for church. It was nice, sitting next to Will in the pretty little community church, singing the hymns she'd known all her life. The sermon was on hope, and she found it uplifting.

Twice Will caught her eye, and they shared a smile. Both times a warm, cherished feeling bloomed within her. She decided that coming to church had been a great idea, after all.

After the service, they lingered awhile. Jordyn introduced Will and the Stevaliks to the pastor and to various members of the local Traub, Dalton and Strickland families. Then Myron and Pia went across the street to the doughnut shop, and Jordyn and Will drove to Kalispell to stock up on groceries for the week ahead.

That evening at Cece and Nick's, Rita and Charles Dalton joined them. The Daltons had five grown children, including the twins Kristen and Kayla. Before the evening was through, Jordyn and Will had an invitation to next Sunday's dinner at the Dalton ranch north of town.

Monday came, and Jordyn realized that her life on the ranch had a nice rhythm, a productive routine. She went to work. And when she came home, she helped Pia clean out and organize the barn. She fussed over the goats and the kittens, and had dinner with Will.

It was good between her and Will. They got along great.

Tuesday, as usual, she and Will had their breakfast and dinner together. They discussed her day's work and his progress at the ranch. They laughed together. He teased her, and she joked back.

They were just like any married couple, she thought, except that, at the end of the evening, they went to bed in separate rooms. She was starting to see that if there was a baby, she and Will would get along together just fine. They could have a good life, build a family, be happy. She just knew that they could.

They were actually pretty well suited, she decided—*very* well suited, as a matter of fact. Her confidence increased that they could make it work.

And if there was a baby, well, then they could be together in every way. She would finally find out what it was like to make love with a good man. It wouldn't be her dream come true exactly, but close enough.

Definitely close enough.

Wednesday very early, she woke up with an ache in her lower belly. She tried to ignore it. But it was a familiar sort of ache, a definite cramping feeling.

She turned over, closed her eyes and willed the feeling away.

It refused to go.

Finally, she sat up and threw back the covers. Even in the dim light just before dawn, she could see the blood on the white sheet.

Her period had started.

So much for having to make it work with Will.

Chapter Ten

Something was bothering Jordyn.

Will noticed it first at breakfast on Thursday. She was too quiet, and she seemed preoccupied. He asked her what the matter was. She said it was nothing, so he took her at her word.

She went off to work.

When she got home, he was still outside with Myron, putting together a lean-to to protect the goats when the weather got bad. He didn't see her until dinnertime, when she was even more withdrawn than she'd been at breakfast.

After the meal she went outside for a while—probably to spoil the goats and pet the kittens and make sure the ornery rooster had enough feed. He wandered into the living room and turned on the TV. By nine she hadn't come in to join him, or even checked in to say good-night.

That bothered him. Even if she didn't hang with him, she always told him good-night before she went upstairs.

He turned off the TV and sat there in the quiet for a few minutes, listening for a sound of her. Nothing.

So he got up and circled the first floor. She wasn't down there. He went outside, checked the barn and the goat pen. No sign of her. She must have gone up to her room without a word to him.

Back inside, the dryer alarm buzzed. He went in the utility room, pulled open the dryer door and found a load of clean sheets.

Might as well take them up to her. It was as good an excuse as any to try to talk to her again, to find out what had happened to make her start acting like a ghost of herself.

Jordyn closed her laptop and tossed it down beside her on the bed. Enough with pretending to do homework. She was too crampy and miserable to concentrate.

She really should go back downstairs and give Will the big news that she *wasn't* having his baby. She should have told him this morning. Or over dinner.

But she hadn't. She was putting it off because…

Well, she didn't know why, exactly. She only knew she felt low and depressed, and she didn't want to talk about it. Hormones, probably. Or so she kept telling herself.

She was just about to go take another painkiller to knock the cramping back a little when he tapped on the door.

"Jordyn? You awake?"

She just sat there for a second or two, staring at the shut door, considering pretending to be asleep.

But come on. She'd been blowing him off all day, and she needed to snap out of it.

"It's open," she called. The door swung inward.

And there he stood, his arms full of her sheets. "Thought you might want these."

She had others, and he knew it. He'd come upstairs to check on her, to find out why she kept saying she was fine, and then dragging around like something awful had happened—and somehow, the sight of his coaxing smile and worried eyes made her feel more depressed and miserable than before.

"Come on," he said. "I'll help you fold them."

She just sat there, looking at him, thinking how manly and handsome he was, wishing...

What?

She really didn't know what she was wishing. Just that things could be different, somehow.

"Jordyn?" He crossed the threshold, dropped the big wad of sheets on a chair and kept coming until he stood by the bed.

She heaved a giant sigh and patted the mattress.

It was all the invitation he needed. He sank down beside her, swinging his stocking feet up onto the comforter next to hers. "Okay. So, what's up with you?"

How to tell him? How to explain this bizarre, depressed state she'd fallen into because there wasn't any baby? She should be overjoyed. After all, they'd only ended up married by accident, and they had a Divorce Plan. They were not what they pretended to be when other people were watching.

"Jordyn, come on. What's up?"

She blew out her cheeks with a weary breath. "Good news?" Somehow, it came out as a question.

"If the news is good, how come you look like somebody died?"

She pressed her fingers to her temples and rubbed in a vain effort to ease her sudden headache away.

He caught her wrists in either hand and gently pulled

them away from her face. "Talk to me. Tell me what's eating at you. Give me a chance to make it better."

"You can't make it better—and anyway, it's nothing horrible. It's a good thing, it really is."

"And this good thing is...?" He gazed at her with real concern.

And that did it. He really did care, and he wanted to know. She couldn't hold it in anymore. "I got my period. There's no baby."

For about a half a second, he looked as stricken as she felt. But maybe that was only her imagination. Because a second after that, he said, "Well, that *is* great news."

"Yeah. It's great. Terrific. Wonderful."

He tipped his head and studied her. "What is it? What's wrong? Come on, you can tell me."

She let her shoulders droop. "It's cramps, that's all. And I have a headache..." Not a total lie. If the cramps and the headache weren't all of what had her feeling low, they definitely contributed.

"Come here." He did the sweetest thing then, easing an arm around her, pulling her close. She surrendered to the comfort he offered, curling her tired, aching body into him, resting her head on his strong shoulder. He asked, "You want some aspirin or something?"

She snuggled in closer, breathing in the scent of him, feeling better about everything, just to have his big arms around her. "I'll get something in a few minutes. It's strange..."

"What?" He put a finger under her chin, tipping it up.

She met those gorgeous eyes. "I don't know. I guess I was kind of getting used to the idea that there would be a baby. Is that odd or what? I mean, it was only one night— and that's *if* we actually did anything."

"Not odd," he reassured her. "Not strange. You were

preparing yourself, that's all. In case it turned out we were going to be parents."

"Preparing myself. I guess that's one way to look at it." She dipped her head and snuggled close to him again.

He wrapped his arms tighter around her and rubbed her back. "You'll feel better soon…"

"I know." Actually, she felt better already. His warm hands felt so good, stroking her shoulders, fingers digging in a little to ease out the kinks. And more than the magic he worked with those rubbing fingers of his, just having his arms around her gave her comfort. She could have sat there, snuggled up with him forever. And he didn't seem in any hurry to get away from her, either.

Jordyn closed her eyes…

Will cradled Jordyn close and listened as her breathing evened out into the shallow rhythm of sleep. He thought about the baby that they weren't going to have.

And he knew it was a good thing. The best thing. She had big plans for her life, and a baby would have changed everything.

And he, well, he had a lot of work ahead of him to get the ranch whipped into shape. It was a round-the-clock job, and he hadn't planned to start a family for a few years, at least.

Better for both of them that the marriage would end as they'd agreed. They could go forward with the plan, get divorced in August and get on with their lives.

Still, a certain heaviness dragged on him, a let-down kind of feeling. He must have been preparing himself, too. Getting himself ready to go forward as Jordyn's husband, getting ready to be a dad.

Now it wasn't going to happen. He should be glad about that. Relieved, even.

But instead, he felt a bone-deep sadness.

As though something so precious was not only lost, but had never been.

Jordyn woke alone in her bed the next morning. Will, sweet and considerate to a fault, had pulled the comforter over her before he left.

She sat up against the headboard—and burst into tears.

Which was totally stupid. She had nothing to cry about.

So she tossed back the covers, ran into the bathroom, stripped down and climbed in the shower. She stayed in there, under the hot spray, until the water ran cool.

And when she got out, she felt a lot better about everything. Will was a great guy, and there was no baby and those were the facts.

Time to get on with the plan.

She put extra effort into her hair and makeup, kind of pulling herself together, putting her depression of the night before behind her. Downstairs, she made French toast for breakfast.

Will had two helpings and told her she looked great. "Seems like you feel better today."

She beamed him her brightest smile. "Much better, thank you."

"Cramps all gone?"

She knew he was only being supportive. But still, today was a new day, and she didn't want to talk about her cramps or the lack of them. She realized that maybe she'd shared too much information with the guy.

After all, he wasn't *really* her husband. And she'd gone too far last night, crying on his shoulder because she wasn't pregnant after all, whining about her cramps and her headache, cuddling up good and close, inviting him to rub her back and hold her, and then falling asleep in his arms.

Boundaries were important, and she seemed to be cross-ing them constantly lately, treating Will like she owned him or something, kissing him and cuddling up to him when it was just the two of them, alone, and no displays of affection were called for.

It had to stop. "I'm feeling great," she said. "Honestly."

He gave her a sideways look, as though he wasn't quite sure what to make of her right then. "If you say so…" He sounded doubtful. Like he thought she was faking it, and she didn't feel great at all.

She almost snapped at him that she didn't like his atti-tude. But somehow, she restrained herself. No need to get annoyed over nothing.

It was time to move on, definitely. Time to get out the dissolution papers and fill in all the blanks. She had to stop putting off dealing with them. And she would, as of today.

But where were they, exactly? Had he even given her the ones she needed to fill out? She couldn't remember.

She sent him a covert glance across the table.

He frowned. "What?"

And she just didn't feel like getting into it with him right then. "Nothing, really. Not a thing." They were prob-ably upstairs in her room somewhere.

Before she left for work, she went looking for them. She turned her room upside down in search of them, but they weren't there.

Didn't matter, though. At Sara's, she went on the county website and printed up a fresh copy of all the forms she needed. Back at the ranch that afternoon, before she got going on her homework, she tackled those forms.

They really were extensive. Everything she owned had to be specifically listed and claimed. Had Will started on his yet? He owned a lot more than she did, and it was bound to take him longer to get everything listed, to get all the exact amounts and the numbers of his accounts. She should probably check with him, make sure he was on top of it.

That night at dinner, when they were halfway through the meal, she said, "I started on the dissolution forms today. They're long. They want to know everything you own and its value. I mean *everything*, so that we can each claim what's ours and there's no dispute later. It's going to take a while to fill out. Especially for you, Will, with the land and all the buildings, the cattle, the vehicles, the furniture. It goes on and on."

He shrugged. "I should get going on that," he said, and kept eating.

Really, she ought to get more of an acknowledgment from him that he was on top of it. "So you will, then? You'll get them out and get going on them?"

He swallowed a bite of pork chop. "Isn't that what I just said?"

"You said you *should*, not that you *would*."

"Fine. I'll get going on it."

She sipped from her water glass, pushed her peas around on her plate and tried to figure out why he suddenly seemed so pissed off. "Okay. What's wrong? Out of nowhere, we're in a conversational minefield here."

"Nothing's wrong." He scooped up a big bite of whipped potatoes and shoved it into his mouth.

Lovely. She decided she needed to keep her eye on the prize. The point was to get him going on the papers. "I mean, do you even know where you put those papers? Because I looked for mine and couldn't find them and had to reprint them today at Sara's."

"I know where they are." He said it flatly. "You could have just asked me if you wanted them so bad."

And you could stop acting like a douche, if you don't mind.

Oh, she was tempted to say it. But she didn't. She kept her tone calm and reasonable. "I didn't want to bother you."

"You wouldn't have been bothering me."

"Great. But the point is we need to get back to the courthouse by the thirty-first at the latest. That's two weeks from now. If we get to the courthouse by the thirty-first, then we get our final court date within twenty-one business days…" She shook her head. "Actually, that's cutting it kind of close. I need to be in Missoula by the third week in August. Yes, all right, if I had to, I guess I could come back, just for the hearing. I'd really rather not, though. I'll be busy when I get there, and it's two hours each way, here and back…" She let her voice trail off and waited for him to say something.

He didn't even glance up, but just kept right on eating his dinner.

Will ate the rest of his potatoes.

He finished off his pork chop. He even ate his peas, and he'd never been all that big a fan of peas. He was seriously pissed off at Jordyn about then. She was getting to him, bugging the crap out of him with her phony behavior since breakfast that morning.

What was her problem that, all of a sudden, she had to nag him up one side and down the other about something he'd already told her he would take care of?

Would she ever shut up about it?

No. She kept talking, telling him what he already knew. He'd been there at the courthouse with her. He had a firm grasp of the time frame, and he would hold up his end. There was absolutely no reason for her to keep yammering on about it.

She nagged him some more. "So you need to get on those papers, Will."

He dropped his fork. It clattered against his empty plate. "How many times are you planning to tell me that?"

She gasped like he'd insulted her. "I just want to be sure that you're on top of it, that's all."

"I'm on top of it," he said, in barely more than a mutter. "You can be sure."

"Well, terrific, then. Let's leave it at that."

"Hey. I keep trying to."

"What is that supposed to mean?"

Let it go, he thought. But he didn't. "It means that you *won't* leave it at that. What the hell is it with you today, anyway? You came downstairs this morning with that big fake smile on your face, acting like you and me are strangers or something. And tonight you suddenly just have to tell me twenty times to fill out the dissolution papers. I don't get what's going on with you. And I don't like it, either."

Her mouth was pursed up tight. "Are you finished?"

Was he? Oh, yeah. Pretty much. "Just back the hell off, Jordyn. I don't know what's up with you all of a sudden, but you can stop about the damn papers. When the time comes, I'll have them ready."

"Thank you," she said in a tone that wasn't thankful in the least.

And then she slid her napkin in beside her plate, pushed back her chair and marched from the room. He heard her swift footsteps climbing the stairs, followed by the slamming of her bedroom door.

What? She thought she was punishing him, leaving him all alone downstairs?

Hardly.

He cleared the table and loaded the dishwasher and then he went to his office nook off the entry hall, got out the papers she wouldn't shut up about and sat down to fill them out.

She was right about them, which only served to make him even madder. He had a lot of crap to list and a lot of information to gather. But he kept after it, working well into the night, digging through the documents in his file cabinets and online for account numbers and proofs of sale. By the time he finally went to bed, he had more than half of it done.

The next morning, she was in the kitchen fixing breakfast when he came in from tending the animals. They sat down to eat in a silence as deep as a bottomless well.

He just didn't get it. Wednesday night, when she'd told him there was no baby, she'd been so sweet, reaching out to him for comfort, falling asleep in his arms. He could have sat there on her bed, just holding her, forever. He'd even considered staying there with her, cradling her slim body in his arms through the night, waking up beside her in the morning.

But he'd left her regretfully several hours before dawn.

And then faced her across the breakfast table Thursday morning and wondered what she'd done with the warm, direct, affectionate woman he'd comforted the night before.

Now it was Friday and they were not speaking. By the time she left for work, she'd yet to say a word to him.

He went to his office and worked on the forms for hours—hours he should have been out taking care of business on the Flying C. But by lunchtime, he'd done it. Those forms were ready for that end-of-the-month visit to the Kalispell Justice Center.

Feeling self-righteous and badly treated and madder than ever, he put them back in the desk drawer, grabbed a sandwich and went out to help Myron move cattle from a near pasture to one farther out.

That night at dinner, he kept waiting for her to ask him about the forms he'd spent half of last night and half of today completing. She didn't ask. She didn't say a word to him beyond "Dinner's ready," and "Please pass the green beans."

It was a cold war they were into now. So, all right. He could do that.

Yeah, he was starting to feel crappy about it, and he wasn't all that proud of his part in it. But then, well, maybe they'd been getting in a little too deep with each other, anyway, acting as if they had more going on together than they did. Maybe a little distance wasn't such a bad thing.

They loaded the dishwasher in total silence.

Once that was done, he said, "I'm going into town to the Ace in the Hole to get a beer with my brothers."

"Great." She granted him a smile so cold, it was a wonder her lips didn't crack and fall off. "I'm going into town, too. I want to see how Melba's doing."

"Have fun," he said in a growl.

"I will." Another brittle smile. "You, too."

Will had already left when Jordyn got in her car and headed for town.

She reached the boardinghouse at a little before eight. Inside, Melba greeted her with a hug and then led her to the front parlor so that she could say hi to Old Gene.

"How's married life treating you?" Old Gene asked.

Jordyn played her part. "Never been happier." As the lie passed her lips, she realized it would have been true a couple of days ago.

Melba grabbed her hand and took her back to the kitchen where they had coffee and brownies—chocolate chip–cookie Oreo-fudge brownies, to be specific. They were wonderfully rich and way too delicious. Jordyn ate one and then couldn't resist having another. Sometimes a girl really needed a gooey Oreo dessert.

She told Melba all about the ranch, about the goats and the kittens, about how the place was really coming together.

Melba told her not to work too hard, to take it easy, relax and smell the flowers. "You sure you're doing okay, honey?" Melba asked. She'd always had a sixth sense about what was really going on with people.

Jordyn kept it light. "Nothing wrong with me that another of these brownies won't cure."

"Help yourself."

Jordyn reached for another one as Claire came in carrying baby Bekka. Claire poured herself a cup of coffee and let Jordyn hold the baby.

Bekka was in a good mood, giggling, waving her fat little hands around. Jordyn cuddled her close and kissed her plump cheek and tried to ignore the sadness that plucked at her heartstrings.

The sadness made no sense, really. But still, she felt it, and strongly—a sadness for the baby she wasn't going to have, the baby she'd somehow started to love and want, even though that baby had never actually existed.

She hadn't talked privately to Claire since that afternoon at Sara's when Claire had cried and confided about her husband going home to Bozeman without her. Jordyn wanted to ask if Claire had heard from Levi, but somehow, the moment never seemed right.

Claire asked, "Did you see last Sunday's edition of the *Rust Creek Falls Gazette*?"

When Jordyn said she'd missed it, Melba filled her in. "The mystery gossip columnist reported that a certain Kalispell detective is looking into the possibility that someone doctored the wedding punch on the Fourth of July."

Jordyn kissed Bekka's cheek again. "Any speculation as to who that mysterious someone might be?"

Melba and Claire both shook their heads. Claire said, "So far, not a clue."

Eventually, Bekka started fussing, and Claire took her off to get her ready for bed. Reluctant to return to the empty ranch house, Jordyn hung around. She asked Melba how Claire was doing.

Melba shook her head again. "About the same, I'm afraid. I keep hoping Levi will show up, or at least get in touch, that the two of them can make up. So far, though, it hasn't happened."

Jordyn's thoughts—as they too often did—turned to Will. "I guess sometimes people say things they shouldn't— hurtful things. And then they let their pride keep them from apologizing and working things out."

Melba patted her arm. "I know they love each other. I stay focused on that, and I don't let myself get discouraged. Real love takes hard times, too. Real love is like faith. It grows stronger when it's tested."

Jordyn sighed. "Melba, that's beautiful. I do believe you are a philosopher."

"No, just an old woman who's lived a full life." She offered the half-empty plate of brownies. "Go on. Have another."

"I've already had three. They're so hard to resist."

"Then don't. Give in. Enjoy. You only live once."

So Jordyn had another. Melba brought the coffeepot over and refilled their mugs. It was nice. Comforting, to sit there in Melba's cozy kitchen, eating those decadent brownies, chatting about love and life and what was going on in town. She could have sat at Melba's kitchen table late into the night.

But by ten, she knew she was pushing it, keeping the older woman up past her bedtime.

Melba hugged her again at the door. "My best to your handsome husband," she said.

"I'll tell him," Jordyn promised. *That is, if I ever speak to him again.* She ran down the front steps in the gathering twilight and gave Melba a last wave as she ducked into her Subaru.

She started it up and turned the corner onto Cedar Street. The quickest way back to the Flying C was a right turn on Main Street. But she went left instead. The next street was Sawmill, where she should have gone right. She turned left again.

Two blocks later, she turned into the parking lot of the Ace in the Hole.

Chapter Eleven

Will nursed his second beer and wondered what he was doing there.

His brothers played pool and flirted with the waitresses and seemed to be having a really good time. Will wasn't. He kept thinking about Jordyn, wondering if she was enjoying her visit with the old lady who ran the boardinghouse.

Wondering if maybe he'd been a little too hard on her. She was right, after all. They had a plan, and the plan included the necessity to fill out the damn divorce papers. He'd needed to get on that. And when she'd first brought it up to him, he *had* blown her off. Could he blame her that she kept after him?

When he got home, if she was there and still up, he would apologize to her for being a horse's ass. Maybe he could even get her to open up and talk to him about why all of a sudden she had to treat him like some stranger, why she had to give him fake smiles and cold, distant looks.

And if she wouldn't open up about what was really going on with her, well, so what? She didn't owe him the secrets of her heart.

He was her husband, yeah, but not in the deepest, fullest way. And not forever. They got along great most of the time. He loved having her around. She was different than any woman he'd ever been with. She took care of business, never slacked. And until the other morning, she'd always been straight with him, always spoken right up and said what was on her mind.

She didn't cling—or maybe, it was more that, when she did cling, he liked it. He liked feeling needed by her, which, with any other woman, always made him want to move on. Plus, she was quick-witted and funny and easy on the eyes.

But what they had together was stamped with an expiration date. And he had no right to blame her for maybe wanting to keep him from getting too close.

Over at the pool table, Rob looked up from taking a shot. His right eyebrow inched toward his hairline as he tipped his head at the arch that led to the main bar. Will followed the direction of his brother's gaze.

And saw Jordyn, in the same snug jeans and purple tank top she'd been wearing when he'd left her in the kitchen hours before.

Jordyn. Damn, she looked good.

All of a sudden, the night brimmed with promise. The music sounded better, the lights shone brighter.

And then he started wondering what she was doing there. Had something gone wrong?

He set down his beer and went to her.

She spotted him—and her eyes got bigger. Softer. Her lips parted slightly. She looked breathless. Excited.

Like she was really glad to see him.

Like he was the only guy in the room.

He eased his way through the crush to get to her. "Jordyn."

She tipped up that sweet face to him. "Will. I, um…"

"Are you okay? Did something happen?"

"No. No, nothing. I mean, nothing *important*. I mean, well, it's…" Her beautiful mouth trembled in the most endearing way. "I don't know. I was at Melba's. And then I was going back to the ranch—but I didn't. I came here instead. And then I drove up and down the rows of cars in the parking lot until I saw your pickup. And then I parked and told myself I wasn't going to come in here…"

He needed to touch her. So he did. He cradled the side of her head, ran his hand down the silky length of her shining hair. And she didn't jerk away—the opposite.

She stepped even closer. "I…well, I was feeling bad, you know? For getting all up in your business over those papers."

He gave it up. "I was a jerk."

And she admitted, "I was a nag."

He took her arm. "Come on. Let's go home."

She hung back. "But your brothers…"

"Don't worry about them. They're having a good time."

"Won't they wonder where you disappeared to?"

"Rob saw you. He watched me come for you. He'll tell them we went home together."

"I wasn't going to ruin your evening…"

"Jordyn. You haven't ruined my evening."

"Honest?"

"As far as I'm concerned, the evening's finally looking up."

A glowing smile bloomed. "You mean that?"

"Damn straight—now stop dawdling. Let's go."

She dawdled some more in the parking lot. He wanted her to ride with him, and she didn't want to leave her car.

Finally, he gave in. She followed him home.

They pulled into the yard twenty minutes later and parked side by side beneath the half disc of the silver moon. He got out fast and went to open her door for her, taking her hand and pulling her up from the driver's seat.

And into his waiting arms.

"Will…" She was sounding breathless again. Her eyes glowed silver, reflecting the moon. "At breakfast yesterday, when I acted so distant?"

"Yeah?" He smoothed her hair again. It was silvery, too, in the moonlight, and so soft and warm.

"I'd started thinking we were getting too intimate, you know? That we needed boundaries."

"Yeah, I get that. I can see why you would want to back off, after Wednesday night…"

She nodded. "When I told you that there wouldn't be a baby?"

"Yeah?"

"I felt so close to you, then, Will. I loved the way that you were with me, the way you held me and rubbed my back. The way you comforted me…"

"But?"

"Well, but then in the morning, I got scared."

"I should have been more understanding. I see that."

She made a soft sound low in her throat. "And I should have been more honest, should have told you that I was scared, instead of putting up walls."

"Jordyn, it's okay."

Those moon-silvered eyes searched his face. "It is? Really?"

"Yeah."

"So then, we're good again, you and me? We're friends again?"

He wanted to be a lot more than just her friend. But he

would take what he could get. As long as she didn't shut him out, didn't treat him like some stranger. "Yeah," he answered in a rough whisper. "We're friends again."

"Oh, Will. I'm glad. I don't like it when things aren't right between us."

What was it about her? The light in her eyes, the way she somehow managed to be shy and bold at the same time. She was something, all right. She was one of a kind.

She slid her hand up to his shoulder and then around his neck. Her soft fingers threaded up into his hair. "And can you maybe...?"

"Maybe, what?"

"Ahem. Um..."

He coaxed her, "Come on. Just say it."

"I, well, I like it when you hold me, Will. I like it when you kiss me. We only have so much time, you and me, together. You know?"

His chest felt suddenly tight, and his heart had set to beating hard and deep. "I know."

"I don't want to waste it. I don't want only to have your affection when someone is watching. I want..." She chickened out.

But by then, he was more than willing to help her along. "Do you want me to kiss you, Jordyn Leigh?"

She swallowed, nodded. "Yeah. That's what I'm asking. That's what I want." She tipped her chin higher, offering those soft lips to him. "Kiss me, Will."

It was the best offer he'd had since the last time he kissed her, an offer there was no way he was going to refuse.

So he gathered her closer, and he lowered his mouth to hers. He started out slow and careful, brushing his lips back and forth across hers.

Until she sighed and opened.

And then he settled his mouth more firmly on hers, settled and went deeper, stroking his tongue across the edges of her teeth, meeting her tongue, which was shy at first but swiftly grew bolder. She tasted so good, and she smelled so sweet. She felt like heaven in his arms, and he wished he would never have to let her go.

He lifted his head. She gave a small moan of protest.

Until he lowered his mouth again, slanting it the other way, and kissed her some more.

Off in the distance, a coyote howled. That ornery rooster answered, crowing at the moon.

And the next time he lifted his head, she smiled up at him dreamily, her eyes full of stars. "We should go on inside."

He made a low sound of agreement. She stepped free of her car door, and he pushed it shut. Then, their arms around each other, they turned for the house.

Inside she made popcorn the way they both liked it, in a pan on the stove. She drizzled it with melted butter. He put ice in two tall glasses and filled them with ginger ale. They went into the living room, where they settled on the sofa. He pulled her in snug against his side. She kept the popcorn bowl in her lap.

He grabbed a handful. "What do you want to watch?— wait. Don't tell me. Something romantic."

And she laughed. "No, I think tonight we need something with car chases and stuff getting blown up."

That surprised him. "You're joking."

"Car chases, Will. And at least a couple of really big explosions."

He shrugged. "If that's what you want, I can definitely set us up with that."

They streamed a thriller. And even with bombs going off and tires screaming, she fell asleep in the middle of it.

When it was over, he picked her up and carried her upstairs.

She woke up as he was carefully putting her down on the bed. "Hey…"

"Shh. Sleep."

She reached up, wrapped her arms around his neck and whispered, "Sleep *with* me…"

He answered honestly. "That's probably more temptation than I'm ready for."

She gave a happy, sleepy laugh. "I'm tempting?"

He groaned. "Do you really need to ask?"

"That's a yes, right?"

He pressed his forehead to hers and nodded. "That is definitely a yes."

She sighed. "But what if we slept the way we did at the Manor, you on the outside, me under the covers."

He'd never had a better offer. "I need to turn the lights off downstairs and brush my teeth."

"That's okay. You promise you'll come back, though?"

He kissed her cheek. "You have my solemn word."

When he returned, in an old pair of sweats and a T-shirt, with an extra blanket under his arm, she was coming out of the bathroom, her face scrubbed clean of makeup. She smelled of toothpaste and had changed into a giant yellow shirt with Bad as I Wanna Be printed across the front.

He put his arm around her, herded her to the bed and waited while she climbed in, scooted to the far side and settled the covers over herself.

"Right here." She fluffed the pillow next to hers.

So he stretched out beside her and settled the blanket over himself. "Happy now?"

"I am, yes." She turned off the light. "Night, Will."

"Sleep tight, Jordyn Leigh."

* * *

Deep in the night, Jordyn woke.

Will was wrapped around her, his big arm settled in the crook of her waist. She didn't move, hardly even let herself breathe.

It felt so good, so right, to be lying in the dark with him. *Special*. That was the word for it.

A slow smile spread across her face. Yes. That was it. It was special, what she had with him.

He was special.

All these years, she'd been waiting for that special someone.

Who would have guessed that her special man would turn out to be Will?

The next morning at the breakfast table, she couldn't get enough of just looking at him. She tried to do it subtly, when she thought he wouldn't notice.

But apparently, subtlety was not her strong suit.

It wasn't long before he demanded, "What?"

She took her time chewing a bite of toast. "Hmm?"

"You keep giving me these strange sideways looks."

"Huh? Me?" She spread on a little more elderberry jam. "This jam is so good, don't you think?" She took another bite. "Delicious."

"What is going on?"

"Nothing." She assumed her most innocent expression.

He peered at her suspiciously. "You're sure?"

"Positive. Eat your eggs."

"You're doing it again, Jordyn."

It was Saturday night. They were in Kalispell, at a Mexican restaurant that served killer guacamole. Earlier, they'd bought the groceries for the week.

Jordyn was thoroughly enjoying herself.

She dipped up a chipful of guacamole and answered innocently, "I have no idea what you're talking about." She stuck the chip in her mouth. "Yum."

He accused, "You keep staring at me."

"No, I don't."

He set down the chimichanga in his hand without taking a bite of it. "Something is going on with you."

She grabbed her margarita, stuck out her tongue and licked the salt along the rim. Will watched her do it. His eyes grew a bit glazed. She loved that. "I'm out with you. I'm having fun. *That* is what is going on with me."

He grumbled darkly, "Uh-uh. There's more."

"Honestly. You are such a suspicious man."

"You *do* keep staring at me. You're planning something, aren't you? You disappeared in the store for at least five minutes. And then, when you popped up again, you had this smirk on your face."

"I do not smirk."

"Yeah. You were. You were smirking. Where did you go?"

"I had to pick up a few things."

"What things?"

She gave him her sweetest smile. "Will, come on. Think about it. What in the world would I be planning?"

He picked up his chimichanga again. "Never mind. I don't even want to know."

Back at the ranch, they put the groceries away.

Then he said he had some bookkeeping to do in his office.

She suggested, "I'll wait up for you."

His dark brows drew together. "Uh, no, better not. It's going to take me a while."

She knew exactly what he was doing—trying to get away from her before she asked him to sleep with her again. And she *did* want him to sleep with her again. She wanted to wake up in the middle of the night with him curled around her.

But she decided not to push it. It was a lot of fun teasing him, and she wasn't quite ready yet; hadn't quite worked up her nerve to make a real move on him. They didn't have forever, but they still had more than a month left together. She didn't need to rush it.

Plus, well, she wasn't exactly experienced at seduction. Better to take it slow, kind of feel her way into it—or at least, that was what she told herself. It sure beat admitting that she had no idea what she was doing, and if she put herself out there, he might just turn her down.

She told him good-night and went on upstairs where she had a nice, juicy romance loaded up on her laptop.

The next day, Sunday, they caravanned to church with the Stevaliks again. Jordyn sat next to her temporary husband as she had the Sunday before. She tried to control her need to keep sneaking adoring glances at him.

She didn't do all that good of a job. Twice he caught her looking at him. The second time he mouthed, "What?" at her.

But she only smiled sweetly and turned her gaze toward the altar again.

That evening they went to the Dalton ranch north of town for dinner. Cece and Nick were there. So were the Daltons' identical twins Kristen and Kayla.

As always, Kayla was shy and subdued. She hardly said a word the whole evening. Kristen laughed and charmed them all with stories of how she'd played a stripper in a little theater production of *Sweet Charity*. Jordyn found herself wondering again, as she had that night at the Italian place in Kalispell, if Kristen might actually be the mystery columnist behind Rust Creek Ramblings.

After the meal but before dessert, Cece dragged Jordyn out on the front porch for a private word.

"You look happy, Jordyn Leigh. You kind of have a glow, you know?"

Jordyn gave her lifelong friend a nudge with her elbow. "Okay. I know you're hinting at something. Just tell me what's on your mind."

"Well, I was kind of wondering if maybe there wasn't a little Clifton on the way?"

Jordyn groaned and made a show of rolling her eyes. "Cece. Come on. We've barely been married for two weeks."

"Sometimes babies come right away."

Jordyn shook her head. "Uh-uh. Not happening." She said it with complete self-assurance, and tried very hard not to think about the baby she hadn't been pregnant with, after all. "Where did you get such a crazy idea?"

"I don't know. It was just…something in your expression every time you looked at Will tonight. Something happy, and a little bit secretive, too. I started thinking maybe you had an idea you might be pregnant, but you hadn't told anyone yet."

Jordyn longed to confide in her friend, to tell her that, if she had a glow, it had nothing to do with babies. If she had a glow, it was all about how she'd finally found that certain special guy. And he just happened to be her husband.

For the next month or so, anyway.

But she didn't feel right about confiding in Will's sister. She didn't want to put Cece in the middle of her Divorce Plan with Will. Later, months from now, she knew she was going to have to come clean with her lifelong friend.

Not now, though. Now she and Will had an agreement, and she wasn't going to drag anyone else into it.

They got back to the ranch at a little after nine.

The minute they were in the door, Will started in with all the things he just had to do. "I really should check on the animals and then put in a little more time on the books..."

She almost threw herself into his arms. But then, at the last second, she chickened out. She told him good-night and let him go.

It was the same the next night and the night after that.

Will always had things he just had to do in the evening. Jordyn went upstairs by herself both nights. He went outside to check on the animals, and then he locked himself in his office. She read and did homework and told herself that tomorrow night she was making her move.

Wednesday night, as usual, he went back outside after dinner. Feeling like a complete coward, she watched him go. She finished wiping down the counters and trudged upstairs, where she called her mom. They chatted for half an hour or so—about the ranch and the progress she and Will had made there, about what was going on down in Thunder Canyon.

After the phone call, Jordyn took a bath, a long one, during which she gave herself a good talking-to. She needed to tell Will what she wanted from him. The days were slipping by, and she didn't have forever to make something happen with her special guy of choice.

If he turned her down, so be it. At least she'd know that she tried.

When she left the bathroom, she heard the TV going in the living room. For once he wasn't holed up in his office. She paused at the top of the stairs and looked down at her worn pink sleep shorts, pink cami and the fat pink socks on her feet. Not an outfit made for seduction.

But she knew that if she ran back into her bedroom to look for something sexier, she might stay in there all night, dithering over what to wear.

Uh-uh. She was making her move, and she was making it now.

She descended the stairs slowly, partly out of terror at the prospect of trying to seduce her husband when she had minimal experience at tempting a man, and partly because she was so nervous that if she didn't watch it, she might trip herself and fall. She would end up sprawled in the front hall with a broken bone or two. Talk about a mood wrecker.

Somehow, she made it to the base of the stairs without incident, even though her knees wobbled and her hands trembled on the banister all the way down.

The front hall opened onto the living room. She could see him, sitting on the sofa, his back to her, facing the TV mounted over the fireplace. He was watching that comedy show where four friends challenged each other to perform embarrassing pranks in public places.

She hovered there, her hand on the newel post, staring at the back of his head and his broad shoulders, at his long arms stretched wide across the back of the sofa. His hair looked wet, and he wore that old gray T-shirt he liked to sleep in. He must have had a shower after he came back inside.

Perfect. They were both nice and clean. Always a good thing when you were going to have sex—especially for the first time.

And good gravy, what was wrong with her? She needed to make her feet move, needed to go into the living room and begin the seduction. But her feet refused to budge.

The seconds ticked by. And she couldn't stand it anymore.

If she couldn't get herself to go in there, maybe she could get him to come to her. She sucked in a big breath and called, "Will!" It came out really loud.

His black head whipped around, and he spotted her standing there clutching the newel post. "Jordyn?"

"Hey." She gave him a weak little wave. "Would you turn off the TV and come here for a minute?"

She totally expected him to shake his head and go back to watching one of the pranksters slather a middle-aged lady in sunscreen.

But he didn't.

He switched off the TV, dropped the remote on the coffee table, got up and came toward her. She watched him getting closer, her breath frozen in her throat, her pulse roaring in her ears. "What's up?"

Before he could sense what she was up to and step back, she reached out and caught his hand.

He blinked and looked down at where she touched him. "Jordyn?" He said her name with way too much suspicion.

Now or never, Jordyn Leigh. Somehow she made herself move at last, stepping up nice and close to him, wrapping his arm around her, settling his hand on her lower back.

A muscle twitched in his jaw, and his eyes grew unfocused. "Jordyn, I…" He seemed to have no clue where to take it from there.

Fine. She was ready for that, ready to lead the way. She was done dithering. Tonight she would take her chances and find out once and for all if there was any hope that her special guy thought she was special, too. "Will."

"Uh, yeah?"

"Sleep with me tonight."

His expression was not encouraging. "Jordyn, I…"

Disappointment felt like a lead weight in her belly. But

she wasn't giving up yet. She slid her hands up that amazing chest of his and twined them around his neck. "Please."

He made a low, pained sound. She only continued to stare hopefully up at him. Then he said gently, "You know, it might be a better idea if we didn't make a habit of that."

A habit? Idiotically, she asked, "A habit of what?"

He sighed. Heavily. "Of sleeping together."

She got it then. "Wait. You're thinking I meant that literally. Sleep as in *sleeping*, the way we did Friday night, and when we stayed at the Manor? And you don't want to *just* sleep with me?"

"Yeah," he said bleakly.

"You want...*more* than just sleeping?"

He looked away, muttered her name again, "Jordyn..."

She realized she needed to try to be at least a *little* seductive. So she stroked her fingers up into his hair with her right hand as she trailed the left back down to his chest, where she traced the crew neck of his shirt with a finger that only shook the tiniest bit. "So you're just going to leave me alone every night with a hot romance novel and my shower massager?"

His mouth fell open. It was so cute when he did that. "I don't believe you said that."

"Just because I'm a virgin doesn't mean I don't have *needs*—and then again, we don't even know if I'm actually a virgin, do we? That ship might have sailed without either of us even realizing it."

A low groan escaped him. "What are you *doing*?"

No going back now. "Let me make this crystal clear. It's not really sleeping I'm after from you, Will."

His whole body stiffened. He gaped down at her. "I... but...you..." Apparently, he didn't know where to start.

She needed to help him. So she said it outright. "I *want*

you, Will." And then she watched, mesmerized, as understanding finally dawned in those gorgeous blue eyes.

"This…" The word died in his throat. He swallowed, hard, his Adam's apple bouncing in an agitated manner. "It's been about sex, hasn't it?" he accused. "That's why you've been staring at me constantly for the past five days."

She felt suddenly defensive. "Oh, come on. A few glances now and then? That hardly amounts to staring at you constantly."

"You know what I mean." He said it through clenched teeth.

She traced the neck of his shirt again. His skin was hot, silky. And he always smelled so wonderful. And wasn't his breathing just a little bit agitated?

Maybe they needed to get more comfortable. She let her finger trail out onto the rock-solid bulge of his shoulder and down his arm, continuing the light caress all the way around behind her to his hand. She captured his fingers. "Come on. Let's sit down." She turned from him and dropped to the bottom step.

He loomed above her, his fingers still caught in hers. "Give me a minute."

Her face was just level with his groin. She glanced down from the hot look in his eyes and directly at the big bulge in his faded jeans.

That did it. She couldn't help it. She let go of his hand as she blushed and looked away, thoroughly embarrassed—and also gravely disappointed in herself.

For a moment there, she'd been feeling reasonably grown-up and more or less in control of the situation. "I…I'm sorry." She planted her face in her hands. "Ugh. Don't listen to me. Clearly, I have no idea what I'm doing."

A silence. Followed by a definite, if somewhat pained, chuckle.

She kept her hands over her eyes. "Now you're laughing at me. I hate you, Will Clifton."

"No, you don't. You like me. A lot."

"Now you're smug. I might have to kill you."

She still had her head in her hands, but she felt the air stir as he dropped down beside her. A low groan escaped him as he sat. That gave her at least a little satisfaction, that his jeans were too tight—and she was to blame.

"Jor-dyn…" He said her name in a singsong, the way he used to do when she was six and he was eleven.

"Don't you make fun of me," she grumbled.

And then he touched her, catching a hank of her hair and guiding it behind her ear, causing goose bumps to skitter across her skin.

"Go away." She nudged at him with her elbow.

"Jor-dyn…" Now his lips were there, touching the shell of her ear, his warm breath fanning across her cheek.

She shivered a little in pleasure, at the feel of him so close. But she still refused to look. "Leave me alone."

"Uh-uh. You started this." He kissed the words into her hair and then breathed against her temple, "And I'm not backing off until you actually talk to me." His hot fingers closed around her wrist. "Come on, look at me…"

She gave up and lowered her hands. "Fine." She turned her head and glared at him. "What do you want from me?"

He kissed the end of her nose. "You're so cute."

"Cute is not what I was going for."

"Then what?"

"More like smokin' hot and completely irresistible."

He looped an arm across her shoulders and pulled her in snug against her side. "Take my word for it. You're doing great."

She let herself lean into him. For a moment they just sat

there. It was nice, actually. Companionable. Easy, but with that little edge of excitement, the thrill of banked desire.

And then he said, "Talk to me. Tell me exactly what you're thinking."

She realized there was nothing to do but give it up. "Remember the morning we woke up married?"

He grunted. "That is a morning I will never forget."

"I told you that I wasn't *saving* myself for marriage..."

"Yeah." His voice was lower now, with a certain tempting roughness to it. "I remember that, too. You said you were saving yourself for someone special."

She straightened a little and looked right at him. "That would be you, Will. You're special to me. I want you to be my first."

He just stared at her. She couldn't tell if he was thrilled—or trying to figure out a way to let her down gently.

She forged ahead. "Look, I get it. I do. I know we're not forever. You have your goals, for your ranch, for your future. I have mine. At the end of August, I'm outta here."

"Wait."

"What?"

"You're saying that no matter what happens between us, the plan doesn't change?"

"That is exactly what I'm saying. I'm saying that this, with us, is just this beautiful, magical *accident* that happened, you know? Somebody did something to the punch, and we ended up married. For a while."

"But—"

She cut him off, sternly. "Will you let me finish, please?"

He scowled. "Go ahead."

"I want you to know that I have loved it, Will, this time with you. Loved every minute of it, even the rocky parts, even when we were barely speaking to each other—and you know what?"

"I'm afraid to ask."

"Well, too bad. I'm telling you, anyway. I say, so what if it's not forever? Life's too short and time goes by. What matters is this. I know that, with you, making love will be beautiful and every kind of exceptional I've been hoping that my first time might be. No, I don't remember much about our wedding night, but right now, I'm totally conscious. And I choose *you*, Will. I do. I choose *you*."

His face changed. His mouth and his eyes got softer somehow. He said in a rough whisper, "Jordyn, even if something *did* happen in that bed at the Manor that night, it doesn't count, and we both know that. You don't have to—"

"Shh." She pressed the tips of her fingers to those soft lips of his. "So now you know for sure why I've been sneaking looks at you, what I've been thinking about. Now I've told you, and you can think about it, too."

His lips moved beneath her touch. "My God, Jordyn. How will I think about anything else?"

She could have sat there on that stair with him all night long. But no. She'd stated her case, and she needed to give him the space to make a choice of his own. She rose. "How about this? We'll sleep on it, okay—separately?"

"Sleep," he groaned, rising to stand with her. "Like that's gonna be happening."

"Good night." And she made herself turn and start up the stairs.

She got exactly two steps before he reached out and pulled her back.

Chapter Twelve

"Don't go." He tugged her down off the stairs and around to face him again.

Her heart was going like a trip-hammer. Still, she managed to rise on tiptoe and brush a kiss against the sculpted line of his scruffy jaw. "Well, okay, then."

He gazed down at her, eyes full of questions—and heat. So much lovely heat. "You're sure?"

She didn't waver. "I am."

"You're not going to wake up tomorrow and regret…"

She put her fingers to his lips again, felt his warm breath flow down her palm. "No. I won't regret it. Ever." Her eyes filled.

He saw her tears, shook his head. "Now you're crying."

She sniffed. "It's kind of a big moment, Will—an *emotional* moment."

He lifted a hand, brushed the back of a finger down the curve of her cheek. His touch burned her, right down to the center of her. How did he do it? The man just set her on fire. "You're certain that it's what you want?"

She gazed up at him steadily. "Yeah. You and me. Lovers. I don't know how to make it any clearer than that."

He stroked a hand down her hair. And then, with the hot, rough pads of his fingers, he traced a path down from her temple, along her cheek and lower, down the side of her throat. It was a light, skating touch. And still, it seemed to lay a brand beneath her skin. "You're so beautiful."

"No."

"Yeah."

"Laila is beautiful." Her sister Laila had actually been a beauty queen.

"*You're* beautiful." He said it gruffly that time. "Stop arguing with me." His hand was on the move again, tracing the line of her jaw, sliding beneath her hair to cup the nape of her neck. He cradled her head, and then he bent closer.

Until their lips met.

Oh, my, that kiss! It curled her toes inside her pink socks, set the butterflies loose in her belly, made her whole body ache in the most delicious way.

She let out a small moan of protest when he lifted his head.

He said, "My bed."

Her mouth went dry as the Great Salt Lake. "Um. Yes. Okay. Your bed, Will—but I need to, um, run upstairs first." He just stared down at her, waiting, burning her with those eyes. She cleared her tight throat. "Ahem. I have condoms. And, er, lubricant…" His mouth twitched. He was trying not to smile. "What is so funny?" she demanded.

"Saturday," he said, "in Kalispell. When you disappeared in the supermarket…?"

"That's right. I bought them then. Just in case I ever got up the nerve to put a move on you."

"I've got condoms."

"But what about lubricant? I mean, we might not need it, but then again…"

He gave in. "Fine. Go get it."

She started to turn—but changed her mind, whirled back and grabbed his hand. "You should come with me. We shouldn't be apart now. One of us could start having second thoughts."

He held his ground. "I'll be right here waiting for you. If you don't come back down, I'll understand."

She hesitated.

He pulled his hand from her grip, took her by the shoulders and pointed her at the stairs. "Go."

"But I want you to come with—"

"Go." He was not budging.

She went—taking off up the steps at a run, reaching the upper floor in seconds, darting into her room, grabbing the tube from the nightstand drawer and racing back to the top of the stairs, where she paused and looked down to see if he'd changed his mind.

He was still there, still waiting below, just as he'd promised.

Their eyes met and locked. Heat coiled low in her belly. Her skin felt electrified, little sparks of sensation firing along every nerve.

He didn't seem to be going anywhere, so she hovered there above him, pulling herself together, allowing herself a deep breath or two.

And then, slowly, with dignity, she descended.

When she reached him, she stepped right up nice and close. "Ready," she told him.

And he moved so swiftly, reaching for her. She was high in his arms before she realized he was lifting her against his broad chest. "Oh!" She grabbed him, wrapping her arms around his neck and holding on tight.

"Kiss me again," he commanded.

She lifted her lips to him. He took them, his hot tongue spearing in, laying claim to her mouth—and more. Everything: her mind, her body, all of her senses, as he carried her past the living room and into the master suite.

He set her down on the thick rug by the wide bed. The room was dim, with only a slant of light falling across the floor from the front hall.

"Here." He held out his hand. She put the tube in it. He set it on the nightstand and switched on the bedside lamp.

She couldn't hold back a tiny gasp of dismay.

He asked, "Too bright?"

The lamp cast a soft, pretty glow across the expanse of the bed. Still, a shiver went through her at the thought of being naked with him. The light might be low, but still, he would be able to see everything. She longed to be brave and tell him to leave it on.

But it was all too new and scary. "I think for this first time…could we have it off?"

"That'll work. Let me turn back the covers first?"

"Okay." She waited while he folded the blankets down. Everything seemed strange and unreal, suddenly. She wasn't having second thoughts, exactly. But she didn't feel all that confident, either.

And then, at last, he reached out and flicked the switch again. The lamp went dark. But light still bled in from the hallway.

He was watching her face. "Darker?"

She whispered, "Yes, please."

He went over and shut the door. And it was better. There was her racing heart, her yearning body. All of her senses had gone on red alert. But the darkness helped. It was one less source of extreme stimulation. The tightness in her belly eased. She felt safer, somehow.

She heard him come back to her as her eyes began to adjust. Slivers of moonlight shone around the sides of the plain cotton curtains that had been there when they moved in.

He was a tall, broad shadow before her.

And then he touched her, gathering her into him, sweeping an arm down to press her lower body against him.

Hard. All of him.

She sighed, a slightly ragged sound. But even with her nerves on a razor's edge, the feel of him was heaven.

And then he kissed her, a slow, tender kiss. As he kissed her, he gathered her cami by the hem. "Lift your arms..." His kissed those words across her lips.

She did what he told her to do. His fingers brushed upward along her sides, creating lovely shivers of sensation. For a moment the cami came between them.

But only for a moment. Then it was gone into the darkness.

Her sleep shorts came next. His thumbs slid in at the flare of her hips. And he pushed them down until they dropped to the rug.

She stepped free of them, kicking them away. And that was it, all it took to undress her. She stood by the bed wearing only her warm socks.

He kissed her some more, wrapping her up in those steely arms of his.

"You, too," she dared to whisper against his mouth. "Your shirt, your jeans..."

He smiled against her lips. And he took her hands and placed them at the sides of his waist. She got the message, getting hold of his soft, old shirt and sliding it up over his hot, hard flesh. He raised his arms for her, and it was off.

She tossed it into the darkness. He took off the jeans himself. She heard the zipper go down, felt him moving in the darkness beside her, bending, kicking free of them.

When he rose to his height again, she reached for him, laying a palm over his heart, trailing it lower. Dark, silky hair grew in a line along the center of his chest. She knew where it led, but she didn't quite have the confidence to follow it the whole way.

He seemed to sense her shyness and clasped her shoulders. "Jordyn…"

"Uh, yeah?"

"Get on the bed. Lie down." He said it softly, gently. And so calmly. So completely in command.

In command.

She smiled a little to herself, thinking of all the years she'd known him, of how she'd always felt she had to resist, make a stand, whenever he tried to take command.

Well, not now. Not here, in the dark, with both of them naked. Tonight she *wanted* him leading the way, needed him in control.

And that struck her as funny. She let out a silly, squeaky laugh.

He pulled her against him. Oh, he felt good, so good. His body pressed to her body, without a stitch to separate them. He whispered against her hair, "You think this is funny?"

"I do," she whispered back. "And I'm nervous."

He caught her chin, tipped it up and kissed her—tenderly at first, but then more firmly, more deeply. She gave herself to that kiss, all the while aware of her bare breasts pressed to his hot chest, of his hardness poking at her belly, his big arms around her.

When he finally let go of her mouth, laughing was the last thing on her mind.

"Lie down on the bed," he instructed for the second time.

And this time she didn't hesitate. She dropped to the mattress, swung her legs up and stretched out, reaching up to position a pillow under her head.

He came down with her, taking her mouth again, kissing her for the longest time, only breaking that wet, open contact long enough to slant his mouth the other way— and kiss her some more.

As he kissed her, he touched her, light caresses, controlled. Careful.

His care helped her, relaxed her. She could feel his erection against her thigh. It seemed very large. But she tried not to think about that yet, tried not to focus on where all this kissing and touching was leading.

He didn't seem to be in any hurry to get to the scary part.

On the contrary, he was kind of feeling his way over her body, exploring her, slowly. Deliciously. As though he had all the time in the world just to touch her. His hands were rough from outside work. Rough in a wonderful way. She welcomed every brushing caress.

The first time he ran his palm across her nipple, she moaned.

"You like that?" he breathed across her cheek.

"Oh, yes, I do."

"More?"

"Please…"

His big hand settled, claiming and molding her breast. It wasn't a large breast. He completely engulfed it. "Perfect," he whispered against her parted lips.

"Uh-uh, they're too small." The words popped out, and she wanted to yank them right back.

"They're perfect," he insisted.

She smiled against his mouth. "Tonight you seem to be saying all the right things."

He brushed his lips back and forth across hers. "Just tell me, okay? Tell me what feels good and what doesn't."

"Okay…"

He flicked her nipple.

She moaned.

"Is that a good moan?"

"It is. It definitely is…"

His mouth had left hers. She wanted to order him to kiss her some more. But then she realized that he *was* kissing her some more. He was trailing those soft, clever lips of his over her chin, down her throat, pausing to lightly suck her skin against his teeth.

It felt really good, and she told him so.

So he continued kissing her. He took one breast in his mouth and then the other, doing wonderful things to them, so that she gasped and moaned and cried, "Yes! Like that, Will. Exactly like that… Oh, don't stop!"

He did just what she ordered him to do—and more. His hand skated down, stroking, caressing as it went, lighting her up like a firecracker, making her sizzle and burn.

And then he touched her. *Really* touched her. She gasped when he did that.

And he asked, "Okay?"

"Okay," she whispered. And then she groaned. "Don't you dare stop."

"Yes, ma'am." He parted her gently. Already, she was very wet. And then he eased one finger in.

Oh, it was wonderful. Better than when she did the same thing to herself. Better because she trusted him and at the same time, there was an element of surprise and of the deliciously forbidden to all this. And oh, the feel of him, the heat of him, the size and the power in his big, male body. He was all around her, touching her, holding her...

She wasn't a complete innocent with men. Now and then, she'd fooled around a little when she really liked a guy. But it had never been like this. She'd had nothing this intimate, this amazing. Not ever in her life before.

It was a first in the most wonderful way.

He slipped that finger in and then another, and he moved them in and out. At the same time, he used his thumb in just the right spot. His mouth stayed at her breast, drawing on it.

She felt the shimmer building within her—so good, so right. With Will, of all people.

Seriously. Who knew?

She barely remembered her earlier nervousness. All she felt was his big body bending over her, his mouth on her breast, his hand at the core of her, stroking her, a third finger gently easing in. She moved her hips, rocking. And he went on caressing her.

And then, just like that, hardly even expecting it, clutching his head to her breast and crying out, she came.

"Rest," he said several minutes later, in a low, rough rumble.

She still felt a certain glow, a sense of complete well-being. By then, her breathing had evened out again. She started to argue, "But I'm not tired and I want..."

He silenced her with a finger against her lips. She smelled her own musky scent. My goodness. The room smelled of sex.

She couldn't help it. She smiled in delight at the thought.

"Rest," he whispered again. "It's just you and me in this house. Nobody's going to bother us. We have all the time in the world."

All the time in the world...

No, they didn't have that, not really—not in the grand scheme of things. Yes, they had weeks yet before their marriage ended and she went off to Missoula. Weeks together. But it was all zipping by much too fast. His lips brushed her temple, his breath stirring her hair.

She just had to ask, "But what about you? Aren't you feeling a little—"

"Jordyn, I'm fine."

"You're not going to explode or anything?" For that, she got a strangled sound from him. She grumbled, "Don't you laugh at me."

"Okay, baby…"

"Will. You just called me *baby*."

"You don't like that?"

She considered. "No, I do. I think I really do."

"Well, okay, then—and no, I'm not going to explode. Or anything." He pulled the covers up over them.

For a little while, trying her best to be obedient—which they both knew was not her forte—she made herself just lie there beside him in the dark.

But there was no way she could sleep. Not yet. She was much too excited. Much too curious, too…captivated. She'd waited so very long for this night with this man. She had zero regrets that she'd waited.

But no way was she stopping now.

"Will?"

"Rest, Jordyn."

"I've been thinking."

He chuckled, the sound a lovely, low rumble. "Somehow, I'm not the least bit surprised."

"I want to see you. But I'm still not all that comfortable with *you* seeing *me*. So I'm thinking, you can shut your eyes and promise not to peek. And I'll turn on the light."

"You're not going to rest, are you?" He didn't sound all that upset about it.

"Uh-uh. Are your eyes shut?"

A silence, then, "Yeah."

"No cheating."

"Promise."

There was a lamp on her side of the bed, too. She clutched the sheet to her chest and felt her way up the base until she found the switch. Soft light pushed back the shadows.

She glanced at Will over her shoulder. He was on his back with his eyes closed, as promised. He had the covers up to his chest. She admired the sculpted perfection of his neck and shoulders, the totally tempting sight of all that tanned, healthy skin against the white sheets. "No peeking," she warned.

He tried to hide his grin. "Clear on that."

"I'm just going to peel back the blankets."

He said nothing, but his lips kept twitching.

So she pulled on the blankets, easing them down— all the way down, finally pushing them into a wad at the footboard.

Will didn't move.

And oh, my. The view was absolutely splendid. He was all hard planes and lean, strong muscles. And still aroused, so she didn't have to suffer performance anxiety over how to get him interested again.

And he looked just as large as he'd felt. She was no expert, but he seemed pretty darn big to her. She could definitely get a little performance anxiety over that, given her likely virginity and all. But then again, he was a man, and she was a woman, and the thing to remember was that the two of them were born to fit.

"Oh, Will…" She bent close to him and rested her forehead against his. "Do you believe we're doing this?"

He didn't speak, just moved his head in one slow pass from side to side.

She took the lead, kissing him, starting out slow the way he'd done with her, brushing his lips with hers, nipping his lower lip, waiting for him to open to her before dipping her tongue inside. After a little while, he reached up and banded his wonderful arms around her.

And after that, she couldn't have said who was running things. He touched her all over. And she grew bolder, even daring to reach down and wrap her fingers around him. He felt like heaven, so silky. Rock hard.

He groaned into her mouth, and then he curled his hand around hers. He showed her how he liked it, which was a lot harder and faster than she would have guessed.

And then, when she sensed he was just on the edge, he caught her hand and muttered a bad word under his breath. She took that to mean he didn't want to come that way.

And that was all right with her, because he instantly began caressing her again, parting her, stroking her, bringing her right to the point where she knew she would go over.

"Wait," she moaned. "I want…"

He made a low, growling sound and swore some more.

She pleaded, "Condom, Will. Please. I want you, all of you."

For once, he didn't argue. "Drawer," he groaned. "My side…" He let her go, and she took one from the box in the drawer and got it out of the wrapper. And then he whispered to her, guiding her, as she rolled it down over him.

She grabbed the tube of lubricant off the nightstand. "Hold out your hand."

He obeyed. She squeezed a little onto his fingers and then onto hers, and then she stroked it on over the condom.

He groaned as she smoothed it on him, at the same time

rubbing his thumb over the shiny drops on his fingers, spreading them. "It might be better if you were on top and in control," he suggested, eyes still shut as he had promised her, dark, thick lashes lustrous against his tan cheeks.

"Yes. Me on top. I think that would be perfect."

A ragged sound escaped him—but then he said gently, "All right, then."

She eased a leg over him and rose to her knees above him. He touched her then, adding the lubricant, making her wetter, slicker, more eager than ever. She rocked her hips in time with his fingers, loving every knowing stroke.

"Whenever you're ready," he whispered, sounding calm, but with a definite edge.

She drew in a long, slow breath and wrapped her hand around him, loving the way his hard belly tightened even more at her touch. Rising higher on her knees, she guided him into place. Carefully, she began to lower herself onto him. "Oh!" She froze, hovering above him as her body resisted. Already, he was stretching her. And he was hardly in at all.

"You okay?" He groaned the words.

"I...need a minute."

"We have all night." It was sweet of him to say that. But the look on his face betrayed him. That look said he was burning to get on with it. She had no doubt that this moment was as agonizing for him as it was for her. But then he whispered, "Easy. It's okay..." And he touched her again.

It helped, his caress. He knew right where she needed the stimulation. She let her head fall back and closed her eyes, sighing, as her body eased and opened around him. The discomfort passed. Heat coiled in the center of her and then began to spread, relaxing her further, and exciting her at the same time. It started to feel good again, to have him there, slick and hard and ready, almost inside her.

She wanted more. She wanted to be filled with him, joined with him, moving on him.

By slow degrees, she pressed down, taking him, pausing every time it started to hurt. Even the ache of him stretching her had a certain promise to it as they waited together, both of them breathing hard, for her body to accept him and welcome him deeper.

At the last, when they were almost there, he grasped her hips in his two hands and pulled her down to meet him.

"Will…" She groaned his name.

"Okay?"

"Oh, yes…"

"Good."

"Yes…"

He took her shoulders and pulled her down to him and pressed a string of kisses along the curve of her cheek. He nipped her chin, licked the tender skin along the side of her throat. Finally, he claimed her mouth again. She opened for him eagerly.

It lasted forever, that kiss.

Her hair fell all around them, and he gathered it up and smoothed it down her back, stroking it, then tangling his fingers in it.

Oh, it was glorious, the taste of his mouth, the breadth of his big body beneath hers, his hands in her hair, the first-in-a-lifetime feeling of him filling her below.

She began to move. Or maybe he moved first. Who could say for sure, and what did it matter, anyway? She only knew that it worked for her, to lift and come down to him, lose him and claim him again, while he let her retreat and then brought her close once more, his hands on her hips now, guiding her, holding her, making it so very good for her.

He kept his eyes closed, as promised. And the longer

he moved inside her, the more dishonest it seemed to hide from him in any way.

"Will?"

He made a guttural questioning sound.

"Would you...look at me now?"

Those black lashes swept up. And she was staring into all that blue. "Beautiful." He said it like he meant it.

She closed her eyes in pleasure and rocked on him faster, feeling her body gathering, shimmering, hitting the peak. With a cry, she went over, throwing her head back as completion cascaded through her.

And then he was sweeping his fine, rough hands up to her waist, lifting and turning her, so he was on top. Those blue eyes burned down at her. "Don't...want to hurt you..."

"You won't," she managed to whisper, though the fading waves of her climax still shuddered through her. "You never could..."

He pushed up on his fists then and powered into her, hard and fast. It shocked her a little—but she breathed deep and went with it, wrapping her legs around him, riding it out.

And then he came down to her again, gathering her into him, groaning her name. She felt him pulse within her. Oh, that was lovely. Perfect.

All of it, exactly as she'd always dreamed it might be.

She twined her arms around him and held him to her heart.

Chapter Thirteen

Jordyn moved her stuff into Will's room when she got home from work the next day. "Because for as long as we have," she told him, "I want us to be together. *Really* together."

Will knew he shouldn't let her do that, just as he shouldn't have said yes to her the night before. It was wrong to get in so deep with her. Wrong for her, because she needed to move on and follow her dream. She didn't need him dragging her back.

Wrong for him, because making love with her and sharing his room with her only made it harder to imagine letting her go. He should have made himself say no.

But he didn't, not when she moved her stuff into his bedroom. And not last night, when she'd asked him to be her first—and no, she hadn't pushed him. She hadn't *had* to push him. She'd just been beautiful and sweet and honest with him, and then asked him to think it over.

There was nothing to think over. Last night he would

have given the ranch he'd finally just got to hold her in his arms all night long.

So he went for it.

And was it worth it?

Oh, you bet.

Maybe he shouldn't have said yes. Maybe he had no right to take what she offered, to be her first.

Too bad.

He'd done it, anyway. And now he intended to enjoy every second he had with her. He was going to love every minute of it and not feel guilty about it.

And when the time came, he would let her go with a gentle word and a smile on his face.

That night when they sat down to dinner, he looked across the table at her and could hardly believe that in just a few hours, they would be together in his bed. She glanced up from her plate of spaghetti, those fine blue eyes sparkling at him.

He decided right then that a few hours was too long to wait.

The minute they had the table cleared, he took her hand and led her to the bedroom. That night was even better than the night before. He didn't have to be so careful not to hurt her. And she was more relaxed, less shy. Plus, they left the light on the whole time, and he got to look at her. Looking at her was almost as good as having his hands on her.

Friday night they made love on the sofa. He missed half the baseball game. And he didn't care in the least.

Saturday at four in the morning, the old billy set up a racket, crying like a baby out in the goat pen. When the aggravating critter kept at it for more than ten minutes, they dragged themselves from the bed, pulled on their clothes and ran out to see what the hell was going on. They got to the pen just in time to watch the nanny deliver a black-spotted kid.

Jordyn made a fuss over the kid—and praised the old billy for calling them out there. The billy talked right back to her, bleating out a cry every time she finished a sentence.

Will grunted. "You know, you shouldn't encourage him."

"But he's a sweetheart, and I *love* him," she argued, and then she told the billy, "Oh, I am going to miss you when I go…"

The billy bleated at her, a pitiful sound, as though he couldn't stand the thought of her leaving.

Will couldn't stand it, either. At that moment, he felt like she'd kicked him right in the gut.

Which was all wrong. What was his problem here? They knew where they stood, and she hadn't said anything he didn't already know.

He turned away to pull himself together. Lucky for him, she was busy playing kissy-face with the goat and didn't notice that he was acting like a fool.

When he could look at her without scowling, he said, "I guess I'll just go ahead and tend the horses, get the morning chores out of the way now that I'm up."

She offered, "I'll help."

"No need." He turned and headed toward the barn and the horse pasture on the far side.

"Will. Wait up!" She came right after him.

He had to restrain himself from turning on her and ordering her to leave him the hell alone. Instead, he stopped and drew in a slow breath and faced her and made himself say calmly, "Go on in and get the coffee started, why don't you?"

She caught her lower lip between her teeth, and he wanted to bite that lip himself, to grab her and kiss her until neither of them could see straight, then to lift her up in his arms and carry her back to his bed.

And never let her go.

She asked in a small voice, "What's wrong?"

Somehow, he pulled himself back from the brink of saying or doing anything too stupid. He schooled his voice to gentleness. "Not a thing. I won't be long."

She studied his face. He knew that look in her eyes. She didn't believe him and she wanted to keep after him.

But miracle of miracles, she let it go. "Okay. See you inside…" And she went.

He stood there in the predawn darkness, watching her walk away, and tried to congratulate himself on not losing his cool over nothing. But congratulations didn't come easy when he just felt like crap about everything.

The weekend went by with a minimum of idiocy on his part. They went to Kalispell for dinner and a movie Saturday night. When they came home, they made love for hours. Sunday night, they had Cece and Nick, Rita and Charles Dalton, and the Stevaliks over for dinner. That got a little iffy for him—because it was so good.

Good to have friends and family and neighbors over. Good to sit at the head of his own dining room table and look at Jordyn Leigh down at the other end. Good to realize that right at that moment, he had everything he'd worked for since he was ten and had decided that one day he would have a ranch of his own.

He'd done it. He had what he'd wanted for so many long years. He had his ranch and a house to call home. And for the moment, anyway, he shared his dream with a woman who had somehow turned out to be everything he hadn't even known he was looking for. Everything he wanted— and she'd been in his life all along.

He watched her chatting with Cece and promising Rita Dalton to help out with the church's summer food drive. And when she passed Myron the vegetables, he had a revelation. She handed over the big bowl piled high with corn on the cob, and Will realized that he'd been waiting all his life for her.

All his life, he'd been moving toward that Saturday four weeks ago, when he'd spotted her at the punch table in Rust Creek Falls Park and couldn't get to her fast enough. For so many years, she'd been too young. And then he'd been too wrapped up in his dream of having a ranch to call his own.

He'd almost missed out. But fate had stepped in. He'd woken up on July 5 married to her.

And now, here they were, husband and wife, sitting at either end of the Sunday dinner table.

There was only one problem. It couldn't last. Because her dream wasn't his dream.

Or did that even matter? Why couldn't she have her dream and be his wife, too?

After all, she wanted him—since last Wednesday, she'd proved that every chance either of them got. And she'd chosen him for her first. Would it be so impossible that she might want him for her one and only?

They got along great and worked together like they'd been doing it all their lives. And when they fought or things got rocky, they worked through it. They got to the bottom of the problem and found a way to resolve it.

She was perfect for him.

And maybe she thought he was all right with her, too. Maybe, just like him, she was sitting down there at her end of the table trying to think of a way to tell him that she didn't want to be his temporary wife anymore. That she wanted those vows they'd exchanged on the Fourth of July—the vows that neither of them could exactly remember—to be legal and binding before God and the world.

For the rest of their lives.

* * *

That night, after everyone left, he was just about to tell her what he felt in his heart.

But then she kissed him. And he ended up doing more showing than telling.

On Monday, as usual, she went off to work in town. He drove into Kalispell to pick up a few things. While he was there, he ran into Elbert Lutello on the sidewalk outside the feed store.

Elbert shook his hand. "How's that beautiful bride of yours?"

"She's amazing," he answered, and meant it.

"The assistant county clerk told me you two came in to pick up dissolution papers." Elbert gave him a stern frown. Before Will could decide how to respond to that, Elbert was all smiles again. "But you never brought them back, so I'm guessing it's all working out for you two love-birds, after all."

"You're right, Elbert," Will replied and refused to feel bad about not revealing the whole truth. "I'm the happiest man alive."

"Excellent. Wonderful. That is just what I wanted to hear. Carmen will be so pleased."

"Tell Her Honor that I said hello."

"I'll do that," Elbert promised.

They shook hands again and wished each other well.

And before he left Kalispell that day, Will took a big step in the direction of claiming what he wanted most. As he drove home, he promised himself that he was going to take his chance. That night, he would make his move.

But then, at the dinner table, she reminded him that they really needed to get over to the Kalispell courthouse by the end of the week and turn in the dissolution papers so that their court date would come before she left for Missoula.

In a cautious tone that set his teeth on edge, she asked, "Um, have you made any progress on getting everything filled out yet?"

That question made his belly burn with acid and his heart beat a sick rhythm under his ribs. He wanted to punch something. "I'll get to it," he told her in a voice that had *back the hell off* written all over it.

She kept after him. "I don't mean to push, Will, but you really need to deal with those. It's a lot of information, and you need to give yourself time to pull it all together."

The damn things were completely filled out and waiting in the desk drawer in his office. He should have just said that, just eased her mind that he'd held up his end.

Instead, he jumped down her throat. "You *are* pushing, Jordyn. Will you back the hell off? I don't need you nagging me."

That shut her up. She pressed her lips to a thin line and just stared at him, big eyes full of hurt and confusion.

He felt like an ass, which made perfect sense because he was acting like one. With effort, he gentled his tone and promised, "I'll have them ready by Friday. Will that do it?"

"Uh, yeah." She forced a trembling smile. "Friday would be great. I'll get the day off, and we'll take them in."

So that pretty much settled it. She'd made it clear what she wanted—for it to go the way they'd agreed from the first. He needed to enjoy the time they had together and let her go without fighting it when the moment came.

A little while later, he apologized for being a jerk about the papers. She kissed him and forgave him. He should have told her he had the papers filled out, but he didn't, though he knew very well that was mean-spirited of him. Somehow, he couldn't bear to admit to her that he had everything ready to make that trip to the courthouse.

Because he *wasn't* ready, and he would never be. And

maybe, deep inside, he kept hoping he would find a way to tell her what was in his heart.

And then, on Thursday while she was still at work, he picked up the mail. It included a fat packet in a big gray envelope from UMT. He could guess what was inside: housing options and meal plans, public transit information—all the student living stuff she needed settled before she started her new life.

In the post office, when he pulled that packet from his box, he had a bad urge to turn and toss it in the wastebasket a few feet away. But what good would that do, except to prove he was a horse's ass?

That packet held the next step on her road to fulfilling her dream. No damn way he would ever do anything to mess with her dreams. He tucked it under his arm and headed for his truck.

At the house, he got out his dissolution papers. He left them on the breakfast nook table for her, next to the college packet. Then he changed his clothes and went out to work.

Jordyn spotted Will in the distance, on the rise above the stock pond, as she drove down the dirt driveway to the compound on her way home from work.

She saw him—and then she quickly turned her eyes to the dirt road again. The sight of him reminded her too sharply that tomorrow was the day. They would go into Kalispell and file the divorce papers.

If he'd filled them out.

But he'd promised her that he would. And he always kept his promises. She needed to stop stewing about it.

What was the worst thing that could happen? He'd fail—for the first time ever that she could remember—to keep his promise. And they would stay married for a while longer.

Staying married to Will…

It was exactly what she wanted.

Only not.

Uh-uh. No. She didn't want him like that. She truly didn't. She didn't want to just wander into staying married because he hadn't bothered to fill out the paperwork that would make them divorced.

She wanted his love. She wanted him to *want* to stay married to her. And she wanted him to say so in no uncertain terms.

But he hadn't.

Then again, neither had she.

And she'd gone not declaring herself one better, now, hadn't she? She'd nagged him about the papers until he'd growled at her to back off. And what message was he supposed to take from that, except that she must be pretty eager to get their marriage over with?

She needed to step up. And she needed to do it right away.

It was only…

What if he said no? What if he told her that he liked her a lot and enjoyed having sex with her, but as far as the two of them staying married, well, that wasn't in his plans? What if he said that he wouldn't be looking for a *real* wife for at least a couple of years yet?

She didn't know if she could bear that—not that he would be so brutal about it. He would find a way to say it gently and sincerely, with kindness and care.

But it didn't matter how he said it; her heart would end up in shreds. She just hadn't managed to buck up and take a chance on a shredded heart. Not as of yet.

And time was running out.

She drove up to the house and parked in the cleared space next to Pia's blue pickup. Inside, she went straight to the kitchen to check on the slow cooker. The pork stew was ready, so she turned the dial to the warm setting and moved on to the breakfast nook table where Will always left the mail.

Her student living packet had arrived.

And right next to it, he'd left a stack of papers.

It took her a moment to process what she was looking at, because suddenly her eyes brimmed with hot tears, and everything went blurry. But then she swiped the moisture away. She could see all too clearly again and had to admit what was right in front of her eyes: Will's dissolution papers.

Her silly hands shook as she picked the damn things up and rifled through them. He'd filled in every blank in his bold, forward-slanting hand.

Damn him all to hell. He'd filled in all the blanks!

She yanked out a chair and fell into it and stared at the papers clutched in her hand. Oh, she did yearn to crumple them up in a wad and throw them in the trash, to tear them to tiny pieces, to strike a match and burn them to cinders.

Which was ridiculous.

She was ridiculous.

It wasn't the papers' fault if Will didn't want to stay married to her.

And, please. How could she even know what Will might want? Had she asked him? Had she gone to him and told him honestly what *she* wanted?

No, on both counts.

Because she was a coward. A ridiculous coward. A wimpy, gutless, chickenhearted fool.

It had to stop. It had to stop right now.

She shot to her feet, dropped the papers on the table and stormed out the back door, banging the screen good and hard behind her. In the goat pen, the billy heard her coming. He set to crying like a baby. For a second or two, she was tempted to take a moment and go to him, to check on the kid, maybe see how Mama Kitty and her brood were doing in the barn.

But no. Uh-uh. No excuses. She was doing this. She was not letting herself back down or be distracted. She was letting the billy cry for now. And the kittens could wait. She'd visit them later.

The ornery rooster strutted toward her. She zipped around him and kept going. He crowed as she went by, but she didn't turn.

Will was no longer in sight up on the rise. She kept going, anyway, clambering over a fence, breaking into a run up the slope, ignoring the cattle that lifted their heads to watch as she raced past.

At the top of the hill, she paused and put her hand to her forehead to block the sun's glare. She scanned the rolling land before her—and spotted him.

He was down below, thigh-deep in the stock pond. He had a rope around what appeared to be a heifer and he struggled, pulling, trying to haul the animal to dry land. Both the critter and the man were covered in mud.

She took off at a run down the slope, wanting to get to him, needing to get it over with at last, to tell him what was in her heart, get it out there between them, whatever the consequences. He had his back to her as he towed on the rope, and he didn't see her coming.

About ten feet from the muddy bank, she halted. Her breath tangled in her throat, her heart beating madly against the walls of her chest. She waited, giving him the time he needed to finish a tough job. She put her hand against her mouth to keep from distracting him as he coaxed and pulled and coaxed some more while the half-drowned heifer stared at him through dazed eyes and bawled in hopeless exhaustion.

He almost had the animal out of the thick mud at the edge of the water when the heifer's legs gave out, and she plopped down with a sad bellow of complete surrender, sending mud flying every which way.

At that point, Jordyn figured she ought to do more than just stand there. "Need some help? I can get her tail."

Will's head whipped around. "Jordyn? How long have you been standing there?"

"Too long. I'll take the tail."

She got exactly three steps closer before he put up a mud-caked glove. "No." His gaze swept over her good jeans and town boots. "You haven't even got gloves."

Right then, the little red heifer, with a loud moo of effort, dragged herself upright again. Will braced with the rope and pulled.

Four steps and the critter cleared the mud.

"Atta girl, there you go." Will piled on the sweet talk as he stepped in close and eased off the rope. The heifer let out another long, tired cry.

And Jordyn's heart was just too full. She couldn't wait another minute. She shielded her eyes to cut the sun's glare and she announced, "Will Clifton, I saw the divorce papers you left on the table, and I am so sorry I nagged you to get them filled out. It was nothing but cowardly of me, to push you to do that. Because the real truth is that filling out those forms is the *last* thing I wanted you to do. Will, I love this ranch. I love our life together, I love the goats and the barn cats, that big nasty rooster—and even that muddy heifer you just pulled from the pond. I love my job and Rust Creek Falls and all the friends I've made here. But most of all, I love you. So, if maybe it's possible that you might feel the same way, I really don't have to go to Missoula. I can take the rest of my classes online just as well. So, I um…"

Was she blowing this?

She feared she might be. Will just crouched there at the edge of the pond, mud all over him, his arm around the heifer's neck, watching her under the shadow of his hat.

Oh, dear Lord, was he trying to figure out a way to turn her down gently?

She wavered in her purpose. And then she caught herself. No way was she backing down now.

If he didn't feel what she felt, well, she'd just have to deal with that. She was through hiding her true feelings, through pretending she wanted to go when she only longed to stay. She was taking a stand, following her heart. And she was doing it now.

Jordyn yanked her shoulders up, hitched her chin high and cried, "Please, Will. I love you. Would you just think about not divorcing me, after all?"

Relief made Will's knees weak. He staggered against the heifer's mud-caked side. Hot damn, Jordyn loved him.

She wanted to stay with him.

He eased the rope off the heifer. He let her go, pushed to his height and slapped her on the rump. She bawled at him. So he slapped her again and gave her a shove. That did it. She staggered forward, found her feet and trotted off, still bawling.

Up the bank, Jordyn hadn't moved. She stood way too still, watching him, her plump lower lip caught between her pretty teeth, her hand shading her eyes.

He took off his hat and dropped it, along with the muddy rope and gloves, right there at the edge of the water. "Jordyn," he said, because his mind and heart were so full of her, he couldn't manage any more at that moment. Just her name. And that was everything.

"Will?" She let her hand drop, and she stared at him, tears filling those big eyes.

"Baby, don't you cry."

"Oh, Will…" And she started crying, anyway.

He lunged up the bank for her. She fell toward him, reaching. He gathered her in. "I'm getting mud all over you."

She gazed up at him, a smear of mud on her chin and tears on her cheeks. "Will Clifton, I do not care about a little mud."

At least his hands were reasonably clean. He wiped those tears with his thumb. And then he kissed her. He put everything into that kiss—his heart, his dreams, all his love. And when he lifted his head, he said, "I love you, too, Jordyn Leigh. And what I want is exactly what you want, for you to stay here on the Flying C and be my wife for the rest of our days."

"Oh, Will. You do? You really, really do?"

"Yeah. I do. I want that more than anything." And then he bent to kiss her again.

But just before his lips met hers, she let out a cry.

He frowned. "Jordyn, what in the…?"

And she pushed him away from her. "Oh, Will. Tell me the truth, now. Are you *sure*?"

His arms were empty again, and he didn't get it. "What the hell, Jordyn. Didn't I just say so?"

She fisted her hands at her sides and tipped her golden head up to the wide, clear sky. "Oh, Will. I know you. I know what a good man you are. And I can't help but wonder if you're just being your usual upright self, just agreeing to stay married to me because it's what *I* want and you believe in the sanctity of the vows that we took—whether either of us can actually remember them or not. I'm afraid you just feel honor bound to stay with me because it's the right thing to do."

Yeah, he loved her. But right then he kind of wanted to strangle her. He muttered, "That was a mouthful you just said, and all of it crap."

She sniffled. "But can you blame me? I won't take advantage of you. I admit that it's tempting. But no. I have to be certain. I have to know for sure."

Will swore. "That does it." He grabbed her hand. "Come on."

"But Will, I—"

He whirled on her and put a finger to her lips. "Jordyn. Wait. I mean it. Not another word."

She gulped. And then she nodded.

And then he turned and started walking, forging up the rise, towing her behind him. He kept going, never breaking stride, down the slope on the other side, through the pasture to the fence. He stopped there and hoisted her up. She got down on her own, and he came over right after, capturing her hand again, leading her through the yard in back.

The billy wailed in the goat pen.

He hollered, "Shut up!"

Damned if that goat didn't actually fall silent. And then that fat rooster strutted right in front of him. He stepped over the rooster and kept on walking.

He didn't even stop on the back step to get out of his muddy boots. He just yanked the screen open, pulled her through and kept going, through the kitchen and the dining room, to his office at the front of the house.

"Stand right there." He positioned her in a splash of sunlight by the window. "Don't even move."

Eyes wide, mouth agape, she did what he told her to do.

He went to the desk, yanked open the drawer and took out the little velvet box he'd stuck in there Monday after his trip to Kalispell. His hands were all thumbs at that point, but somehow, he got that box open and took out two rings.

Jordyn caught on then. A soft gasp escaped her, but she kept her peace. She did not say a word.

And then he went to her and dropped to one knee. "Give me your hand."

Those blue eyes were filling again, but he knew her well enough to tell the good tears from the bad. She held out her hand.

He slid off the cheap band she'd been wearing since that morning in Kalispell when they made their Divorce Plan. And in its place he slipped on an engagement ring thick with diamonds and a matching platinum wedding band.

"Will," she said. Just his name. And it was more than enough. He knew by the sound of her voice that she believed him at last.

He said, "I saw Elbert Lutello in town on Monday."

"No…"

"Yeah."

"What, um, did Elbert say?"

"Just that he knew we'd been in and picked up dissolution papers. But then he assumed we'd decided to stay together because we hadn't brought the papers back. He said his wife would be so pleased to know that we were happy."

She gazed down at him tenderly. "I love you, Will."

He had a boulder-size lump in his throat. He swallowed it down. "After I talked to Elbert, I found the nearest jewelry store and bought this for you."

"Monday," she marveled. "You did that on Monday. And I never guessed…"

"For days now, I've been trying to find a way to ask you to stay with me, to be my wife for the rest of our lives. I *do* want what you want, Jordyn. You're the one for me. I think you always have been. I took one look at you on the

Fourth of July in that blue dress with your shining, pinned-up hair coming loose on your shoulders, and I knew something good was going to happen between us."

Her cheeks flushed with pleasure. And she teased, "I think the doctored punch played a part—and those romance-loving Lutellos, too."

"Maybe a little. But I swear to you on my life, Jordyn, eventually the end result would have been the same—and I don't really care *how* it happened with us. I'm only grateful that it did. I just didn't want to hold you back or keep you from your dreams."

"You're not. Oh, Will. *This* is what I want. You and me and our life, here, together. Yes, I want my degree. And I'm going to get it. I just…don't need to run off to Missoula to make that happen. I was leaving town mostly because I thought I needed a fresh start. And then I woke up married to you—and what we have together has turned out to be all the fresh start I need. So I'm not leaving. I'm staying here. With you."

He got to his feet then. "Jordyn…"

She put her hands on his shoulders. "I goaded you about those papers. I was such a coward. I hoped that when I pressured you, you'd just burst out with how you loved me and you wanted me to stay."

He admitted, "I had those papers ready for weeks."

"No."

"Oh, yeah. But I refused to admit I'd finished them. I was stalling, trying to find the right moment to ask you to stay. And then, Monday night, just when I was about to go for it and whip out that ring, you got on me again about the papers. I took it as more proof that you really did want to go, and I needed to stand down."

She groaned. "We were such a couple of idiots."

He tipped up her chin. "But we're not idiots anymore."

And then he couldn't wait. He swooped down and claimed her sweet mouth, bending to scoop her up in his arms at the same time.

She laughed against his lips—and then went on kissing him as he carried her out of his office, through the front hall, past the living room, into his bedroom and straight to the bathroom for a shared shower to wash off all the mud.

More than washing went on in that shower.

And from there, he took her to bed, where they properly celebrated the end of the Divorce Plan and the beginning of the rest of their lives.

* * * * *

Look for the next installment of the new Harlequin Special Edition continuity

MONTANA MAVERICKS:
WHAT HAPPENED AT THE WEDDING?

Claire Strickland thought she'd found her happy ending with husband Levi Wyatt, but now she and her baby girl are back living at her grandparents' boardinghouse— and it's all her fault! When Levi returns, will they get a chance at a fresh start?

*Don't miss
DO YOU TAKE THIS MAVERICK?
by* USA TODAY *Bestselling Author
Marie Ferrarella
On sale August 2015, wherever Harlequin books and ebooks are sold.*

THIS WAS HER favorite kind of Haven Point evening.

McKenzie Shaw locked the front door of her shop, Point Made Flowers and Gifts. The day had been long and hectic, filled with customers and orders, which was wonderful, but also plenty of unavoidable mayoral business.

She was tired and wanted to stretch out on the terrace or her beloved swing, with her feet up and something cool at her elbow. The image beckoned but the sweetness of the view in front of her made her pause.

"Hold on," she said to Paprika, her cinnamon standard poodle. The dog gave her a long-suffering look but settled next to the bench in front of the store.

McKenzie sat and reached a hand down to pet Rika's curly hair. A few sailboats cut through the stunning blue waters of Lake Haven, silvery and bright in the fading light, with the rugged, snowcapped mountains as a backdrop.

She didn't stop nearly often enough to soak in the beautiful view or enjoy the June evening air, tart and clean from the mighty fir and pines growing in abundance around the lake.

A tourist couple walked past holding hands and eating gelato cones from Carmela's, their hair backlit into golden halos by the setting sun. From a short distance away, she could hear children laughing and shrieking as they played on the beach at the city park, and the alluring scent of grilling steak somewhere close by made her stomach grumble.

She loved every season here on the lake but the magnificent Haven Point summers were her favorite—especially lazy summer evenings filled with long shadows and spectacular sunsets.

Kayaking on the lake, watching children swim out to the floating docks, seeing old-timers in ancient boats casting gossamer lines out across the water. It was all part of the magic of Haven Point's short summer season.

The town heavily depended on the influx of tourists during the summer, though it didn't come close to the crowds enjoyed by their larger city to the north, Shelter Springs—especially since the Haven Point Inn burned down just before Christmas and had yet to be rebuilt.

Shelter Springs had more available lodging, more restaurants, more shopping—as well as more problems with parking, traffic congestion and crime, she reminded herself.

"Evening, Mayor," Mike Bailey called, waving as he rumbled past the store in the gorgeous old blue '57 Chevy pickup he'd restored.

She waved back, then nodded to Luis Ayala, locking up his insurance agency across the street.

A soft, warm feeling of contentment seeped through her. This was her town, these were her people. She was part of it, just like the Redemption Mountains across the lake. She had fought to earn that sense of belonging since the day she showed up, a lost, grieving, bewildered girl.

She had worked hard to earn the respect of her friends and neighbors. The chance to serve as the mayor had never been something she sought but she had accepted the challenge willingly. It wasn't about power or influence—not that one could find much of either in a small town like Haven Point. She simply wanted to do anything she could to make a difference in her community. She wanted to think she was serving with honor and dignity, but she was fully aware there were plenty in town who might disagree.

Her stomach growled, louder this time. That steak smelled as if it was charred to perfection. Too bad she didn't know who was grilling it or she might just stop by to say hello. McKenzie was briefly tempted to stop in at Serrano's or even grab a gelato of her own at Carmela's— *stracciatella*, her particular favorite—but she decided she would be better off taking Rika home.

"Come on, girl. Let's go."

The dog jumped to her feet, all eager, lanky grace, and McKenzie gripped the leash and headed off.

She lived not quite a mile from her shop downtown and she and Rika both looked forward all day to this evening walk along the trail that circled the lake.

As she walked, she waved at people walking, biking, driving, even boating past when the shoreline came into view. It was quite a workout for her arm but she didn't mind. Each wave was another reminder that this was her town and she loved it.

"Let's grill some chicken when we get home," she said aloud to Rika, whose tongue lolled out with appropriate enthusiasm.

Talking to her dog again. Not a good sign but she decided it was too beautiful an evening to worry about her decided lack of any social life to speak of. Town council meetings absolutely didn't count.

WHEN SHE REACHED her lakeside house, however, she discovered a luxury SUV with California plates in the driveway of the house next to hers, with boat trailer and gleaming wooden boat attached.

Great.

Apparently someone had rented the Sloane house.

Normally she would be excited about new neighbors but in this case, she knew the tenants would only be temporary. Since moving to Shelter Springs, Carole Sloane-Hall had been renting out the house she'd received as a settlement in her divorce for a furnished vacation rental. Sometimes people stayed for a week or two, sometimes only a few days.

It was a lovely home, probably one of the most luxurious lakefront rentals within the city limits. Though not large, it had huge windows overlooking the lake, a wide flagstone terrace and a semiprivate boat dock—which, unfortunately, was shared between McKenzie's own property and Carole's rental house.

She wouldn't let it spoil her evening, she told herself. Usually the renters were very nice people, quiet and polite. She generally tried to act as friendly and welcoming as possible.

It wouldn't bother her at all except the two properties had virtually an open backyard because both needed access to the shared dock, with only some landscaping between the houses that ended several yards from the high watermark. Sometimes she found the lack of privacy a little disconcerting, with strangers temporarily living next door, but Carole assured her she planned to put the house on the market at the end of the summer. With everything else McKenzie had to worry about, she had relegated the vacation rental situation next door to a distant corner of her brain.

New neighbors or not, though, she still adored her own house. She had purchased it two years earlier and still felt a little rush of excitement when she unlocked the front door and walked over the threshold.

Over those two years, she had worked hard to make it her own, sprucing it up with new paint, taking down a few walls and adding one in a better spot. The biggest expense had been for the renovated master bath, which now contained a huge claw-foot tub, and the new kitchen with warm travertine countertops and the intricately tiled backsplash she had done herself.

This was hers and she loved every inch of it, almost more than she loved her little store downtown.

She walked through to the back door and let Rika off her leash. Though the yard was only fenced on one side, just as the Sloane house was fenced on the corresponding outer property edge, Rika was well trained and never left the yard.

Her cell phone rang as she was throwing together a quick lemon-tarragon marinade for the chicken.

Some days, she wanted to grab her kayak, paddle out to the middle of Lake Haven—where it was rumored to be so deep, the bottom had never been truly charted—and toss the stupid thing overboard.

This time when she saw the caller ID, she smiled, wiped her hands on a dish towel and quickly answered. "Hey, Devin."

"Hey, sis. I can't believe you're holding out on me! Come on. Doesn't your favorite sister get to be among the first to hear?"

She tucked the phone in her shoulder and returned to

cutting the lemon for the marinade as she mentally reviewed her day for anything spill-worthy to her sister.

The store had been busy enough. She had busted the doddering and not-quite-right Mrs. Anglesey for trying to walk out of the store without paying for the pretty hand-beaded bracelet she tried on when she came into the store with her daughter.

But that sort of thing was a fairly regular occurrence whenever Beth and her mother came into the store and was handled easily enough, with flustered apologies from Beth and that baffled "what did I do wrong?" look from poor Mrs. Anglesey.

She didn't think Devin would be particularly interested in that or the great commission she'd earned by selling one of the beautiful carved horses an artist friend made in the woodshop behind his house to a tourist from Maine.

And then there was the pleasant encounter with Mr. Twitchell, but she doubted that was what her sister meant.

"Sorry. You lost me somewhere. I can't think of any news I have worth sharing."

"Seriously? You didn't think I would want to know that Ben Kilpatrick is back in town?"

The knife slipped from her hands and she narrowly avoided chopping the tip of her finger off. A greasy, angry ball formed in her stomach.

Ben Kilpatrick. The only person on earth she could honestly say she despised. She picked up the knife and stabbed it through the lemon, wishing it was his cold, black heart.

"You're joking," she said, though she couldn't imagine what her sister would find remotely funny about making up something so outlandish and horrible.

"True story," Devin assured her. "I heard it from Betty Orton while I was getting gas. Apparently he strolled into the grocery store a few hours ago, casual as a Sunday morning, and bought what looked to be at least a week's worth of groceries. She said he didn't look very happy to be back. He just frowned when she welcomed him back."

"It's a mistake. That's all. She mistook him for someone else."

"That's what I said, but Betty assured me she's known him all his life and taught him in Sunday school three years in a row and she's not likely to mistake him for someone else."

"I won't believe it until I see him," she said. "He hates Haven Point. That's fairly obvious, since he's done his best to drive our town into the ground."

"Not actively," Devin, who tended to see the good in just about everyone, was quick to point out.

"What's the difference? By completely ignoring the property he inherited after his father died, he accomplished the same thing as if he'd walked up and down Lake Street, setting a torch to the whole downtown."

She picked up the knife and started chopping the fresh tarragon with quick, angry movements. "You know how hard it's been the last five years since he inherited to keep tenants in the downtown businesses. Haven Point is dying because of one person. Ben Kilpatrick."

If she had only one goal for her next four years as mayor, she dreamed of revitalizing a town whose lifeblood was seeping away, business by business.

When she was a girl, downtown Haven Point had been bustling with activity, a magnet for everyone in town, with several gift and clothing boutiques for both men and women, restaurants and cafés, even a downtown movie theater.

She still ached when she thought of it, when she looked around at all the empty storefronts and the ramshackle buildings with peeling paint and broken shutters.

"It's his fault we've lost so many businesses and nothing has moved in to replace them. I mean, why go to all the trouble to open a business," she demanded, "if the landlord is going to be completely unresponsive and won't fix even the most basic problems?"

"You don't have to sell it to me, Kenz. I know. I went to your campaign rallies, remember?"

"Right. Sorry." It was definitely one of her hot buttons. She loved Haven Point and hated seeing its decline—much like old Mrs. Anglesey, who had once been an elegant, respected, contributing member of the community and now could barely get around even with her daughter's help and didn't remember whether she had paid for items in the store.

"It wasn't really his fault, anyway. He hired an incompetent crook of a property manager who was supposed to be taking care of things. It wasn't Ben's fault the man embezzled from him and didn't do the necessary upkeep to maintain the buildings."

"Oh, come on. Ben Kilpatrick is the chief operating officer for one of the most successful, fastest-growing companies in the world. You think he didn't know what was going on? If he had bothered to care, he would have paid more attention."

This was an argument she and Devin had had before. "At some point, you're going to have to let go," her sister said calmly. "Ben doesn't own any part of Haven Point now. He sold everything to Aidan Caine last year—which makes his presence in town even more puzzling. Why would he come back *now*, after all these years? It would seem to me, he has even *less* reason to show his face in town now."

McKenzie still wasn't buying the rumor that Ben had actually returned. He had been gone since he was seventeen years old. He didn't even come back for Joe Kil-patrick's funeral five years earlier—though she, for one, wasn't super surprised about that since Joe had been a bastard to everyone in town and especially to his only surviving child.

"It doesn't make any sense. What possible reason would he have to come back now?"

"I don't know. Maybe he's here to make amends. Did you ever think of that?"

How could he ever make amends for what he had done to Haven Point—not to mention shattering all her girlish illusions?

Of course, she didn't mention that to Devin as she tossed the tarragon into the lemon juice while her sister continued speculating about Ben's motives for coming back to town.

Her sister probably had no idea about McKenzie's ri-diculous crush on Ben, that when she was younger, she had foolishly considered him her ideal guy. Just thinking about it now made her cringe.

Yes, he had been gorgeous enough. Vivid blue eyes, long sooty eyelashes, the old clichéd chiseled jaw—not to mention that lock of sun-streaked brown hair that al-ways seemed to be falling into his eyes, just begging for the right girl to push it back, like Belle did to the Prince after the Beast in her arms suddenly materialized into him.

Throw in that edge of pain she always sensed in him and his unending kindness and concern for his sickly younger sister and it was no wonder her thirteen-year-old self—best friends with that same sister—used to pine for him to notice her, despite the four-year difference in their ages.

It was so stupid, she didn't like admitting it, even to herself. All that had been an illusion, obviously. He might have been sweet and solicitous to Lily but that was his only redeeming quality. His actions these past five years had proved that, over and over.

Through the open kitchen window, she heard Rika start barking fiercely, probably at some poor hapless chipmunk or squirrel that dared venture into her territory.

"I'd better go," she said to Devin. "Rika's mad at something."

"Yeah, I've got to go, too. Looks like the Shelter Springs ambulance is on its way with a cardiac patient."

"Okay. Good luck. Go save a life."

Her sister was a dedicated, caring doctor at Lake Haven Hospital, as passionate about her patients as McKenzie was about their town.

"Let me know if you hear anything down at city hall about why Ben Kilpatrick has come back to our fair city after all these years."

"Sure. And then maybe you can tell me why you're so curious."

She could almost hear the shrug in Devin's voice. "Are you kidding me? It's not every day a gorgeous playboy billionaire comes to town."

And that was the crux of the matter. Somehow it seemed wholly unfair, a serious Karmic calamity, that he had done so well for himself after he left town. If she had her way, he would be living in the proverbial van down by the river—or at least in one of his own dilapidated buildings.

Rika barked again and McKenzie hurried to the back door that led onto her terrace. She really hoped it wasn't a skunk. They weren't uncommon in the area, especially not this time of year. Her dog had encountered one the week before on their morning run on a favorite mountain trail and it had taken her three baths in the magic solution she found on the internet before she could allow Rika back into the house.

Her dog wasn't in the yard, she saw immediately. Now that she was outside, she realized the barking was more excited and playful than upset. All the more reason to hope she wasn't trying to make nice with some odiferous little friend.

"Come," she called again. "Inside."

The dog bounded through a break in the bushes between the house next door, followed instantly by another dog—a beautiful German shepherd with classic markings.

She had been right. Rika *had* been making friends. She and the German shepherd looked tight as ticks, tails wagging as they raced exuberantly around the yard.

The dog must belong to the new renters of the Sloane house. Carol would pitch a royal fit if she knew they had a dog over there. McKenzie knew it was strictly prohibited.

Now what was she supposed to do?

A man suddenly walked through the gap in landscaping. He had brown hair, but a sudden piercing ray of the setting sun obscured his features more than that.

She *really* didn't want a confrontation with the man, especially not on a Friday night when she had been so looking forward to a relaxing night at home. She supposed she could just call Carole or the property management company and let them deal with the situation.

That seemed a cop-out since Carole had asked her to keep an eye on the place.

She forced a smile and approached the dog's owner. "Hi. Good evening. You must be renting the place from Carole. I'm McKenzie Shaw. I live next door. Rika, that dog you're playing catch with, is mine."

The man turned around and the pleasant evening around her seemed to go dark and still as she took in brown sun-streaked hair, steely blue eyes, chiseled jaw.

Her stomach dropped as if somebody had just picked her up and tossed her into the cold lake.

Ben Kilpatrick. Here. Staying in the house next door.

So much for her lovely evening at home.

* * * * *

Don't miss
REDEMPTION BAY by RaeAnne Thayne,
available July 2015
wherever HQN Books are sold.
www.HQNBooks.com

Available July 21, 2015

#2419 Do You Take This Maverick?
Montana Mavericks: What Happened at the Wedding?
by Marie Ferrarella
Claire Strickland is in mommy mode, caring for her baby girl, Bekka. She doesn't have time for nights on the town...*unlike* her estranged husband, Levi Wyatt. The carousing cowboy wants to prove he's man enough to keep his family together, but can he show the woman he loves that their family is truly meant to be?

#2420 One Night in Weaver...
Return to the Double C • by Allison Leigh
Psychologist Hayley Templeton has always pictured herself with an Ivy League boyfriend, but she can't seem to get sexy security guard Seth Banyon out of her mind. Overwhelmed with work, Hayley turns to Seth for relief in more ways than one. She soon finds there's more heart and passion to this seeming Average Joe than she ever could have imagined.

#2421 The Boss, the Bride & the Baby
Brighton Valley Cowboys • by Judy Duarte
Billionaire Jason Rayburn is back home on his family's Texas ranch, looking to renovate and sell off the property. So he brings in lovely Juliana Bailey to help him clean up the Leaning R. Juliana is reluctant to work with irresistibly handsome Jason, who's the son of an infamous local businessman. Besides, she has a baby secret she's trying to keep—at the risk of her heart!

#2422 The Cowboy's Secret Baby
The Mommy Club • by Karen Rose Smith
One night with bull rider Ty Conroy gave Marissa Lopez an amazing gift—her son, Jordan. She never expected to see the freewheeling cowboy again, but Ty is back in town after a career-ending injury forced him to start over. Both Marissa and Ty are reluctant to trust one another, but doing so might just lasso them the greatest prize of all—family!

#2423 A Reunion and a Ring
Proposals & Promises • by Gina Wilkins
To ponder a proposal, Jenny Baer retreats to her childhood haunt, a cabin in the Arkansas hills. To her surprise, she's met there by her college sweetheart, ex-cop Gavin Locke. Years ago, their passion blazed brightly until Jenny convinced herself she wanted a more secure future. Can these long-lost lovers heal past wounds...and create the future together they'd always wanted?

#2424 Following Doctor's Orders
Texas Rescue • by Caro Carson
Dr. Brooke Brown works tirelessly as an ER doctor. She does her best to ignore too-handsome playboy firefighter Zach Bisho, who threatens her concentration. But not even Brooke can resist, soon succumbing to his charm, and a fling soon turns into love...even as Zach discovers his adorable long-lost daughter. Despite past hurts, Brooke and Zach soon find that there's nowhere they'd rather be than in each other's arms...forever!

REQUEST YOUR FREE BOOKS!

2 FREE NOVELS PLUS 2 FREE GIFTS!

⬧HARLEQUIN®

SPECIAL EDITION

Life, Love & Family

YES! Please send me 2 FREE Harlequin® Special Edition novels and my 2 FREE gifts (gifts are worth about $10). After receiving them, if I don't wish to receive any more books, I can return the shipping statement marked "cancel." If I don't cancel, I will receive 6 brand-new novels every month and be billed just $4.74 per book in the U.S. or $5.49 per book in Canada. That's a savings of at least 12% off the cover price! It's quite a bargain! Shipping and handling is just 50¢ per book in the U.S. and 75¢ per book in Canada.* I understand that accepting the 2 free books and gifts places me under no obligation to buy anything. I can always return a shipment and cancel at any time. Even if I never buy another book, the two free books and gifts are mine to keep forever.

235/335 HDN GH3Z

Name   (PLEASE PRINT)

Address   Apt. #

City   State/Prov.   Zip/Postal Code

Signature (if under 18, a parent or guardian must sign)

Mail to the **Reader Service:**
IN U.S.A.: P.O. Box 1867, Buffalo, NY 14240-1867
IN CANADA: P.O. Box 609, Fort Erie, Ontario L2A 5X3

Want to try two free books from another line?
Call 1-800-873-8635 or visit www.ReaderService.com.

* Terms and prices subject to change without notice. Prices do not include applicable taxes. Sales tax applicable in N.Y. Canadian residents will be charged applicable taxes. Offer not valid in Quebec. This offer is limited to one order per household. Not valid for current subscribers to Harlequin Special Edition books. All orders subject to credit approval. Credit or debit balances in a customer's account(s) may be offset by any other outstanding balance owed by or to the customer. Please allow 4 to 6 weeks for delivery. Offer available while quantities last.

Your Privacy—The Reader Service is committed to protecting your privacy. Our Privacy Policy is available online at www.ReaderService.com or upon request from the Reader Service.

We make a portion of our mailing list available to reputable third parties that offer products we believe may interest you. If you prefer that we not exchange your name with third parties, or if you wish to clarify or modify your communication preferences, please visit us at www.ReaderService.com/consumerschoice or write to us at Reader Service Preference Service, P.O. Box 9062, Buffalo, NY 14240-9062. Include your complete name and address.

HSE15

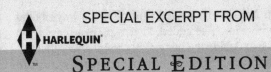
*Claire Strickland thought she'd found The One in
Levi Wyatt. But marriage and a baby put a seemingly
irreparable strain on their relationship. Can Claire and
Levi wrangle a true happily-ever-after with their child?*

*Read on for a sneak preview of
DO YOU TAKE THIS MAVERICK?
by USA TODAY bestselling author **Marie Ferrarella**,
the second book in the 2015 Montana Mavericks continuity,
MONTANA MAVERICKS:
WHAT HAPPENED AT THE WEDDING?*

"You don't mind if I see her?" he asked uncertainly.

"No, I don't mind," Claire answered in the same quiet
voice. She gestured toward the baby lying in the portable
playpen. "Go on, it's okay. Since Bekka lights up whenever you walk into a room, maybe it might be a good
thing for her if you spent a little time with our little girl."

"Thanks," Levi said to her with feeling. Then he slanted
another look toward Claire—a longer one as he tried to
puzzle things out—and asked, "How do you feel about
my spending time with her mother?"

Claire arched one eyebrow as she regarded him. "I
wouldn't push it if I were you, Levi," she warned.

He raised his hands in a sign of complete surrender.
"Message received. You don't need to say another word,
Claire. My question is officially rescinded," he told her.

And then, because he prided himself on always being truthful with Claire, he added, "I'm a patient man. I can wait until you decide to change your mind about that."

Because he had really left her no recourse if she was to save face, Claire told him, "I don't think there's enough patience in the whole world for that."

"We'll see," Levi said softly, more to himself than to her. "We'll see."

Claire gave no indication that she had overheard him. But she had.

And something very deep inside her warmed to his words.

Don't miss
DO YOU TAKE THIS MAVERICK?
by Marie Ferrarella, available August 2015 wherever Harlequin® Special Edition books and ebooks are sold.

www.Harlequin.com

JUST CAN'T GET ENOUGH?

Join our social communities
and talk to us online.

You will have access to the latest
news on upcoming titles and special
promotions, but most importantly,
you can talk to other fans about your
favorite Harlequin reads.

Harlequin.com/Community

Facebook.com/HarlequinBooks

Twitter.com/HarlequinBooks

Pinterest.com/HarlequinBooks

HARLEQUIN®

A *Romance* FOR EVERY MOOD™

Stay up-to-date on all your
romance-reading news with the
Harlequin Shopping Guide,
featuring bestselling authors, exciting new
miniseries, books to watch and more!

The newest issue will be delivered right to you
with our compliments! There are 4 each year.

Signing up is easy.

EMAIL

ShoppingGuide@Harlequin.ca

WRITE TO US

HARLEQUIN BOOKS
Attention: Customer Service Department
P.O. Box 9057, Buffalo, NY 14269-9057

OR PHONE

1-800-873-8635 in the United States
1-888-343-9777 in Canada

Please allow 4-6 weeks for delivery of the first issue by mail.

THE WORLD IS BETTER WITH

Romance

Harlequin has everything from contemporary, passionate and heartwarming to suspenseful and inspirational stories.

Whatever your mood, we have a romance just for you!